Storm at
Daybreak

Also by B.J. Hoff
in Large Print:

The Penny Whistle
Winds of Graystone Manor

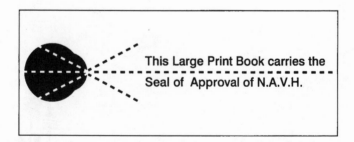

Storm at Daybreak

B.J. HOFF

Thorndike Press • Thorndike, Maine

Published in 1998 by arrangement with
Tyndale House Publishers, Inc.

Thorndike Large Print® Christian Mystery Series.

The tree indicium is a trademark of Thorndike Press.

The text of this Large Print edition is unabridged.
Other aspects of the book may vary from the original edition.

Set in 16 pt. Plantin by Al Chase.

Printed in the United States on permanent paper.

Library of Congress Cataloging in Publication Data

Hoff, B. J., 1940–
   Storm at daybreak / B.J. Hoff.
     p. cm.
    ISBN 0-7862-1317-5 (lg. print : hc : alk. paper)
    1. Large type books. I. Title.
  [PS3558.O34395S7 1998]
  813′.54—dc21   97-39289

AUTHOR'S NOTE

The town of Shepherd Valley, West Virginia, is fictional. The majestic beauty of the mountains and the indomitable spirit of the people are wonderfully real.

My sincere thanks to the Governor's Office of Economic & Community Development and the Chamber of Commerce of West Virginia for their generous assistance.

Thanks, also, to Ms. Catherine W. Swan, The Seeing Eye, Inc., Morristown, New Jersey.

> *He heals the bird with the broken wing . . .*
> *He heals the child with a broken dream . . .*
> *He heals the one with a broken heart . . .*
> *Our Lord makes all broken things whole.*
>
> *— B. J. Hoff*
> *From "Broken Wings"*

PROLOGUE

Patches of ice checkered the pavement, barely noticeable beneath the drifting snow. The driver of a battered pickup swerved when the voice came over the radio, and the rear wheels skidded in response. With an edgy glance in the rearview mirror, he pulled off the highway, bumping and sliding over a frozen mound of snow. When the truck finally pitched to a stop, he let the engine idle as he turned up the volume on the radio.

He hated the voice, but he had to listen. It was important that he listen every day now.

His mouth quivered, and he wiped his hand across it impatiently. Kaine was at it again with his holier-than-thou hogwash.

He has his nerve. Who gave him the right to get on that microphone of his and tell the whole town — the whole country — what to do?

His head was beginning to ache from that fool's incessant yammering. He pushed a hunting cap farther back on his head, then tucked a limp strand of hair underneath it. *Thinks he's funny this morning. A real comedian.* Saturdays were always the worst. Other days Kaine mostly played that church music of his and didn't say much. But on Saturdays

7

he talked a lot more.

Now he was talking about the big radio-thon. The man ran the back of one hand slowly down his leg, snagging a split fingernail on the torn seam of his jeans. He licked his lips, then twisted them in a sneer at his own sour taste.

The voice on the radio made a few more comments about a nationwide campaign to increase drunk driving penalties.

The man snorted. *Something ought to be done about that big, mouthy ape. Got the whole town thinkin' he's so special, so important. Just because he owns a radio station. A* Christian *radio station. Just because he's different, not a normal man. Maybe everybody wouldn't think he was such a prize if they knew. If they knew about my kid.*

He squinted through the icy glaze forming on the windshield, his eyes watering as he listened. *Somebody needs to shut him up. He talks too much. He's got nothing else to do, that's his problem. So he spends his time preachin' over the radio.*

No wife or kids, of course. The man laughed aloud, a sharp, ugly sound. *No woman'd have the likes of Kaine, that's a fact. A woman wants a normal man. He'll never have himself any kids of his own, so he tries to take someone else's boy.*

He pressed his fingertips to his temples, trying to silence the pounding in his brain. *I'm sick of you, Kaine . . . sick of thinking about you, sick of the sound of you. One of these days, somebody's gonna pull the plug on you, shut you up for good.*

ONE

Jennifer glanced around the lobby of the radio station, hoping to see a receptionist. When she didn't, she walked toward the two glass-enclosed studios. A lanky teenage boy with mournful eyes was vacuuming the empty studio on the left. He exchanged a shy smile with Jennifer through the glass partition, then returned to his work.

Catching a glimpse of her reflection in an oak-framed wall mirror, Jennifer stopped for a moment to make a quick inspection of herself. Three hours behind the wheel of her aging Honda had left her feeling rumpled, stiff, and at a definite disadvantage for her interview with Daniel Kaine. She searched the cluttered depths of her shoulder bag for a brush. Finding none, she made a futile attempt to comb her hair with her fingers, then lifted one cynical eyebrow in defeat and shrugged philosophically.

Sensing movement out of the corner of her eye, she turned to the studio on her right. A lone disc jockey was sprawled comfortably in a worn brown chair, adjusting his headset as he spoke into a suspension mike.

The two years she had spent in Rome studying voice with Carlo Paulo had conditioned Jennifer to a steady parade of intriguing, attractive men. While not exactly immune to their appeal, she considered herself difficult to impress. At the moment, however, she was definitely impressed.

He wasn't handsome — at least not in the conventional sense. He had the look of a vagabond prince, Jennifer thought fancifully. A hint of nobility subtly blended with a touch of the maverick. Even slouched as he was with one leg thrown idly over the arm of his chair, she could see that he would tower over her by several inches. At five-eight, she didn't run into that too often.

She moved closer, nearly touching her nose to the glass window. The disc jockey placed one large hand on the control board and the other on his headset to make an adjustment. His red V-neck sweater emphasized the breadth of his shoulders, and his faded jeans made his legs look even longer. His hair was an odd shade of charcoal — not quite, but almost black, a peculiar dusky color. A line of silver winged randomly from his left temple upward, a startling contrast to the thick, dark strands that fell over his forehead.

Jennifer dryly reminded herself that she didn't care for beards, although his was thick and neatly trimmed. His nose was a little too hawkish for her taste, and his shaggy hair could do with some attention. Still, she was intrigued by his profile, and what she could see of his features hinted at a sense of humor and a comfortable, friendly kind of strength.

Unexpectedly, he turned and looked directly at her. She let out an embarrassed groan and backed quickly away from the studio window, briefly registering the disappointing thought that he seemed singularly unimpressed. He hadn't blinked an eye when he caught her staring.

"May I help you, or are you just window shopping?"

The deep voice at her back halted her movement away from the studio. Jennifer jumped, then whirled around to encounter, almost nose-to-nose, a more conventionally handsome man than the disc jockey. His skin was sun-burnished, his blond hair streaked with gold. He wore a winter-white ski sweater, and his green eyes danced with mirth above a remarkably perfect nose and a dark mustache.

Jennifer was beginning to think she had somehow taken a wrong turn and ended up in an employment agency for male models instead of a Christian radio station. She gaped at the life-sized physical fitness ad who was smiling at her.

"Help me?" she stammered in confusion. "No — I mean yes!"

The green eyes twinkled with even more amusement. "Yes, you need help, or yes, you're window shopping?"

Jennifer stared at him. Her recovery time was slower than usual this morning, probably due to lack of sleep the night before. "I . . . I have an appointment for an interview. With Mr. Kaine."

"Ah! Then you must be Jennifer Terry." He offered his hand and continued to smile.

Jennifer adjusted her shoulder bag and drew a long breath of relief as she shook his hand. "Yes, I am."

"Gabe Denton. News director, gofer, and court jester. At your service." He paused. "You're a Buckeye, right?"

His smile was infectious, and Jennifer grinned back. "Yes — Athens, Ohio. Is everyone in West Virginia this friendly?"

"You bet. It's the altitude. You went to O.U., didn't you?" He didn't wait for an answer. "I almost went there, too, but Dan talked me into attending West Virginia U. He's forever talking me into something. I have no backbone, I suppose."

Jennifer's mind reeled from his high-speed verbal barrage. "I see."

13

"I reviewed your resume with Dan last week. He's very interested. Come on, I'll get you a cup of coffee while you're waiting for him. He'll be with you in a few minutes."

He led her down a paneled hallway to the left of the studios, carrying on a constant flow of idle chatter as they went. Turning, they entered a bright, informal lounge where the whisper from a heat register was the only sound. It was a cheerful room with hanging baskets, a floral chaise, and matching chairs. A large commercial coffee urn and a variety of cups rested on a white table.

"Did you drive down this morning?" Denton asked, pouring a cup of coffee that smelled rich and delicious. Jennifer's stomach reminded her with a growl that, in her characteristic rush out of the house, she had skipped breakfast.

"Yes, I left home about seven."

"No one should have to get up that early on Saturday," he said with a sympathetic grimace. "It's criminal."

"Actually, I'm used to it," she said, gratefully accepting the coffee. "Where I'm working now, I have to be at the station by six o'clock every morning except Sundays."

"No wonder you're job hunting." He extended a small plate of cookies to her, and she took a couple. "Well, Jennifer, I hate to desert you, but I have an insurance rep in my office who's expecting a stroke of advertising genius from me. Do you mind waiting alone? I'll go in and tell Dan you're here."

After a quick sip of coffee, Jennifer motioned him on. "I'll be fine. Go ahead. Oh — and thanks for the coffee!"

"It'll be great working with you." Denton gave her a quick wave and turned to go.

"But I haven't got the —," Jennifer stopped, her words trailing off as he dashed out the door.

She carried her coffee over to the window. If the lounge were indicative of the rest of the station, the place was definitely a step up. The small Christian station where she worked now was little more than a two-room warehouse a few miles outside Athens.

She liked the job, but the time had come to move if she were ever to make a dent in the loan her dad had assumed for her music studies in Italy. The salary quoted for this position was surprisingly good, and she was determined to make a good impression on Daniel Kaine.

Not for the first time, Jennifer wondered what to expect of the man who owned and managed the station. She already knew Kaine was young. She remembered what Dr. Rodaven, her former professor at Ohio University, had told her when he first contacted her about the job.

"I've only met the man twice, Jennifer, but I was impressed with him. He's in his late thirties, I suppose. Seems highly intelligent — a fine Christian, too, by the way. I don't suppose you'd remember, but Kaine made quite a name for himself and his community several years ago in the Olympics. He took a gold medal in swimming, as I recall. I watched him on television — a real powerhouse in the water. Great athlete. A terrible tragedy, what happened to him . . ."

"What sort of tragedy?"

"He's blind. There was a car accident a few years ago — a teenager, I think. Drunk driver. Daniel Kaine lost his sight, and I believe the boy died."

Jennifer had nearly backed off then and there. A man with that kind of disability might be expecting someone to function more as a personal aide than an executive assistant. What Jennifer really wanted was to break into management and perhaps have a show of her own. The stark reality of financial need, however, had been enough incentive to lure her to Shepherd Valley for an initial interview.

So, here she was, though not without reservations. She sipped the coffee slowly, gaz-

16

ing out at the winter landscape.

I could learn to love this place in no time, she thought, enthralled by the mountains.

A town of approximately thirty thousand people, Shepherd Valley nestled peacefully at the bottom of a wide range of some spectacular mountains, white now with January snow. The entire community formed an oval, with only a few buildings fanning out into the surrounding woods. Since the radio station sat squarely on top of a hill, Jennifer had a breathtaking view of the Appalachian settlement below. It appeared to be very old and quaint and tranquil.

Her thoughts returned to Daniel Kaine. The only blind person Jennifer had ever known was Miss Rider, the elderly piano teacher she had seen for half an hour weekly while she was still in elementary school; she barely remembered her. What was it like, living without sight, knowing you would never see again?

According to Dr. Rodaven, Kaine's blindness was permanent, caused by severe damage to the optic nerve. Jennifer shuddered, trying to imagine how she would deal with a tragedy like that in her own life. Her mind went briefly to her younger brother, Loren, a victim of cerebral palsy. She had helped to raise him after their mother's death, and even now she felt a sharp twist of pain whenever she thought about the way her brother's condition had ravaged his body and trapped his mind. *Which would be worse,* she wondered, *spending your life in a wheelchair or living in continual darkness?* She pressed her lips together, resolutely swallowing a familiar lump of resentment.

She couldn't stop thinking about Daniel Kaine. Always curious, she turned and placed her nearly empty coffee cup on the white lacquered table beside the chaise. She shut her eyes and stood perfectly still for a moment to fix her sense of direction. Then, slowly and cautiously, she began to walk across the room, her hands flailing out and groping with every step. She felt something fall with a soft thump but refused to give in to the temptation to look. Weaving back and forth, she continued to walk, flinching when she heard something else topple, but still resisting the urge to open her eyes.

She should be close to the door by now. She turned sharply to retrace her steps — and collided so soundly with a hard, massive shape that her head snapped backward from the unexpected blow.

Her eyes flew open to encounter an incredibly broad chest covered with a crimson

V-neck sweater — a chest her hands were now braced against in an attempt to steady herself.

The disc jockey! Her stomach sank with a thud.

Miserably, Jennifer raised her eyes upward, then higher still, to the dark, bearded face lowered toward her with a questioning stare. She felt her face heat with embarrassment.

"Excuse me." The voice was low, richly timbred, with a soft but definite drawl. "Am I, ah . . . in your way?"

Jennifer uttered a small groan of dismay. "Oh — no! I — oh, I'm *so sorry!*"

The big man smiled, and Jennifer had a fleeting memory of a sunrise she'd once seen from her window in Rome — slow and gentle and breathtaking.

"Did I run into you? Or did you run into me?" He laughed easily and continued to stare down at her with wonderful blue eyes.

Startled, Jennifer realized that her hands were still splayed against him. She yanked them abruptly away with a choked exclamation. "I — I definitely ran into you," she stammered. "Did I hurt you? Oh, I feel so incredibly *stupid!*"

Still smiling, he braced one arm above her on the doorframe, trapping her within his

19

space. "You needn't. I run into things all the time."

He was being wonderfully nice, but she felt like such a klutz! Here she was, finally face-to-face with a man who could make her heart go wild, and she was walking around with her eyes closed, for goodness' sake!

"I'm not totally crazy, honest!" she blurted out. "You see, I have an appointment with Mr. Kaine for a job interview, and . . . well, I was waiting for him, and I started thinking about what it would be like, not being able to see. And I — well, I just shut my eyes to try it out for myself, and — oh, I suppose it *sounds* even more stupid than it must have *looked!*"

Jennifer knew she was chattering — she always did when her composure was shaken — but the disc jockey simply kept on smiling, as though he didn't quite know what to make of her.

Running his hand lightly over his beard, he finally spoke. "I don't think that's so stupid," he drawled softly. "In fact, I think it shows a lot of sensitivity."

"You do?" Jennifer stared at him blankly.

He nodded. "Absolutely. You were wondering what it's like to be blind, right?"

"Yes. But my brother told me I should say 'unsighted' rather than 'blind.' What does Mr. Kaine prefer, do you know?"

He appeared to consider her question carefully for a moment. "I don't think he much cares what you call it. So . . . you have an interview for a job here?"

"Yes, as Mr. Kaine's executive assistant. Have you been here long?"

"Mm-hm. A long time. You any good?"

"I beg your pardon?"

"At what you do. Are you any good?"

Really, wasn't he strange? "Well, I think I am. I have a degree in broadcast communications — and experience. What do *you* do?"

His smile was disarmingly boyish. His even white teeth flashed in dazzling contrast to his dark hair and skin as he moved away from the doorframe and took her hand. He placed his much larger hand over hers on his forearm and motioned her to the doorway.

"As a matter of fact, I own the place, Jennifer. Jennifer Terry, isn't it?" he said smoothly as they entered the connecting office.

"Now then, why don't you just come in and sit down, so we can talk. I've got a hunch you're already hired, so we'd better start getting acquainted, don't you think?"

TWO

Jennifer skidded to a stop on the other side of the door, narrowly avoiding a second collision. Her mouth fell open on a sharp intake of breath, and she gaped at him in startled silence. He waited, a trace of mischief scurrying across his features.

"*You're* Daniel Kaine?"

"Guilty." The man had a grin like a jolt of electric current.

She didn't know whether to groan with embarrassment or simply try for a fast getaway. "Well, if you'd only *told* me —," she muttered weakly.

"Told you?"

"Who you *are!*"

He nodded. "Sorry, I guess I got a little . . . sidetracked."

"Well, now that you've seen me make an utter spectacle of myself. . . ."

"I wasn't looking — honest." A dry note of amusement edged his words.

Jennifer slapped the palm of her hand against her head, moaning softly when she realized what she had said. "I'm so sorry," she said miserably, wondering if she would have liked the job.

"Jennifer — sit down and relax, OK?"

His hand still covered hers on his thickly muscled forearm, and he pressed it gently, moving her across the plush carpet to a chair that sat directly opposite a large walnut desk.

Jennifer sat down cautiously. Glancing up, she encountered the curious, dark-eyed gaze of one of the most beautiful dogs she had ever seen. An elegant golden retriever resting casually beside the massive desk studied her with friendly interest.

"What a lovely dog!"

"Ah . . . she likes to hear that, don't you, girl?" Kaine eased his large frame into the chair behind the desk, then leaned sideways to stroke the dog's head affectionately. "Jennifer, meet Sunrise Lady of Shalimar. Her friends call her Sunny."

"Is she —"

"My guide dog," he finished for her. "One of the best — from the Seeing Eye in New Jersey." He skimmed his hands quickly over the right side of the desktop, stopping when he touched a slim file folder. Opening it, he began to run his fingertips lightly across the Braille letters of the top sheet.

The dog sat up, tilted her head to the side, and began to whine softly. "I believe Sunny would like to introduce herself to you," Kaine said, smiling as he continued to read the Braille file.

"Is it all right to pet her?"

He nodded. "It's fine when she isn't working."

Jennifer extended her hand, and the retriever immediately perked up her ears even more, then looked appealingly at her owner.

As though he could see her bid for approval, he inclined his head slightly. "Go on, girl."

Sunny shook off her dignified demeanor at once, bounding over to Jennifer and nudging her hand in an undisguised attempt to get her ears rubbed. Jennifer complied, laughing at the small sounds of pleasure coming from the dog's throat. "How old is she?"

Kaine thought for a moment. "A little over seven. But she thinks she's still a puppy."

He called the retriever back to his side, and the dog returned without hesitation.

"OK, Jennifer, I think I remember most of the information on your resume. Gabe went over it with me a few days ago." Kaine leaned comfortably back in his chair and locked his hands behind his head. "You're twenty-seven?"

Jennifer nodded, then caught herself and spoke. "Yes."

"Born and raised in Athens, Ohio. Nice town," he said thoughtfully. "I was there a few years ago with my teen ensemble. I noticed Carey Rodaven was one of your references. Did you study with him at O.U.?"

For the next few minutes he continued to mix his questions with casual, friendly comments. Jennifer was intrigued by the slow, rambling way he spoke, his words flowing smoothly in a soft Appalachian drawl.

As she listened to his mellow voice, she scrutinized his features. If one could accurately measure a person's character by his face, she would judge Daniel Kaine to be an extremely kind, good-natured man who had known more than his share of trouble, yet had come through it reasonably unscathed. Everything about his appearance, his voice, his mannerisms seemed to fuse together into a unique combination of unshakable strength, patient tolerance, and relentless humor.

He also possessed, she realized uncomfortably, a distinct magnetism. His size, rather than presenting the blustering threat of an aggressive grizzly, held more the endearing appeal of a comfortable, but powerful, giant panda. He appeared to be essentially pleasant; she would guess him to be a man who seldom lost his temper. And something in that youthful, mischievous grin told her he liked to have fun and might even be a bit of a practical joker.

But he also had a blunt, no-nonsense way about him that unnerved her. It occurred to Jennifer that Daniel Kaine would not be easily taken in. She suspected that he possessed the intuitive ability to go straight to the heart, to strip aside any superfluous layers of camouflage and pierce the depths of another's spirit.

It didn't help that his blue eyes — beautiful eyes, Jennifer thought — followed sound and movement and contributed to the overall impression of a highly developed intelligence and sensitivity. It was true that they lacked perfect focus, but this simply gave him a somewhat pensive expression, as though he were continually looking at or listening for something in the distance. When he faced her, Jennifer had the sharp, unsettling sensation that he could *see* her.

Kaine put her file aside and leaned forward, lacing his fingers together on top of the desk. "Why don't I fill you in on the job first, Jennifer? Then, if you're interested, I'd like to hear more about you." He smiled again, seemingly intent upon putting her at ease.

"The job description that was sent to you might have been a little vague," he continued in his soft, mild voice. "What I'm looking for is someone to function as an assistant station manager as well as my executive assistant. Gabe Denton, the comedian you met earlier, has more to do than he can handle. He's our program director and acting sales manager and — well, I've just got to get some help for him. There's a fellow coming in next week to interview for sales manager. If he works out, that will help, but we still —"

The telephone interrupted him with a shrill ring, and Jennifer glanced at the special instrument with its large, raised numerals. "Sorry," Kaine said. "My secretary doesn't work on Saturdays, so I have to pick up my calls. I'll try to make it quick."

Jennifer resisted the urge to study him while he was on the phone — somehow it seemed unfair, almost as though she'd be taking advantage of his sightlessness. Instead, she let her gaze roam over his desk. A large Bible, probably Braille, she thought, lay close to his right hand, and just a few inches away stood a clock with raised numerals and a machine that looked like a small record player. To his left was a battered IBM Selectric, as well as numerous Braille papers. Bookshelves held a state-of-the-art stereo system, and on the opposite wall hung framed photographs of Christian recording stars. Many of the photos, Jennifer noted with interest, included Daniel Kaine. She was trying not to eavesdrop, but when she heard the agitation in his voice and saw his heavy dark brows knit into an annoyed frown, she couldn't help but wonder what was so disturbing about the call.

"Listen —" The soft, gentle drawl she had found so charming moments before now deepened. He sounded almost gruff as he went on. "I don't know what your problem is, but you're not going to solve it like this. If you want to come in and talk, that's fine, but —"

Surprised by his abrupt change of manner, Jennifer was even more puzzled when she heard a loud click at the other end of the connection and saw Kaine hold the receiver away from his ear. He replaced it slowly and quietly, shaking his head in puzzlement.

He managed a brief smile for her before he spoke again. "Takes all kinds, I suppose." He made no attempt to explain what had transpired, and Jennifer didn't ask. "So . . . where was I? Ah — I was interested in the job you're doing now, Jennifer. Gabe said you have quite a variety of responsibilities, that you're doing a little of everything."

"Yes, it's just a small station. Everyone has to be a jack-of-all-trades."

"Well, that could be a real plus around

here," said Kaine. "Things get pretty hectic every now and then. It would help to have someone who could pitch in as needed." He leaned forward a little more.

"Let me explain something else before we go any further, all right?" His pleasant, good-natured smile was back to normal now. "Some people are intimidated by my disability. They simply can't relate to it, so they find it difficult to work for me. That makes it awkward for me, too. I've got to have someone in this job who isn't going to get all strung out about working with a blind man. Someone who'll be comfortable with me — so I can be comfortable, too. We're going to be together too much for it to work any other way. Do you understand what I mean?"

Jennifer considered her answer for only an instant. "I think so. And I've got to be honest with you, Mr. Kaine. I've never worked with anyone who . . . couldn't see. But I don't think it would be a problem for me once I learn your way of doing things."

Kaine nodded slowly, running the palm of his hand lightly across his beard. "Well, let me put your mind at ease about one thing. If you're afraid you'd end up as a nursemaid, you wouldn't. Most things, I do for myself. My little blonde here —" he leaned over to stroke the retriever behind the ears — "gives me a lot of independence I wouldn't have otherwise. And Katharine Chandler, my secretary, keeps me more organized than I'd like to be. I'm sorry you couldn't meet her today, by the way. She puts in so many hours through the week, I don't think it's fair to ask her to come in on Saturdays, too."

He crossed his arms over his chest, and his massive shoulders reminded Jennifer that the man had been an Olympic swimmer. She forced her attention back to his voice.

"I have a housekeeper to keep my place from turning into a condemned area. And I also have an overprotective sister who takes care of my social life — such as it is." He flashed his annihilating grin and pushed his chair even farther away from the desk.

"And, of course, I have Gabe. He's my right-hand man. And my best friend. He's also the best program director in the state." Another smile darted across his face. "Gabe's sense of humor leans a bit to the odd side every now and then, but he's a great guy. He's also my part-time chauffeur and drives me to and from the station every day. Anyway, I've got all the personal attention I need — sometimes more than I can handle. What I *do* need is an assistant with some smarts and a healthy dose of common sense who can also take my blindness in stride." He paused for just a moment. "Since you've been working for a Christian station, I assume that you have some church background."

"Yes," Jennifer assured him. "I'm a Christian."

He nodded. "Good. Everyone who works here is. We try to function primarily as a ministry. Of course, we have to make a profit to pay the bills, but we try to keep our priorities straight. Did you grow up in the church?"

"Yes. My grandfather was a minister," Jennifer explained. "In fact, he started the church my family attends."

"With your background in music, I imagine they keep you real busy singing."

Jennifer swallowed hard, not answering for a moment. When she finally spoke, she deliberately kept her tone even and bland. "Actually, I don't sing anymore."

Kaine raised one dark brow. "Not at all?"

"No."

Jennifer waited tensely for the question he seemed about to ask, but after a brief hesitation, he simply smiled and changed the subject. "Well, now it's your turn to ask questions."

Relieved, Jennifer leaned forward a little.

"What exactly would my responsibilities be?"

Kaine lifted a hand with an encompassing motion. "Helping me run the place, mostly. You'd coordinate programming with Gabe, do some public relations for us, cover a lot of the community stuff — you know, concerts, church activities, civic meetings, that sort of thing. I said you wouldn't be a nursemaid, but you *would* be driving me around some, I'm afraid. Would you mind that?"

"Not at all," Jennifer answered quickly.

"Good. I would need you to get going on one thing right away. We're the coordinating station for a nationwide radiothon coming up in just a few weeks. Gabe and I have been working on it for months, but we keep getting bogged down in other stuff. Consequently, we're not nearly as far along as we should be with the planning."

"What kind of radiothon?"

"We're hoping to generate more public interest and awareness regarding drunk driving laws. There's been a good deal of improvement, but too many people are still indifferent to the problem. It takes financial support, political pressure — we'd like to stir up some enthusiasm for both." Kaine hesitated a moment, then went on. "I was asked to coordinate the effort because of my

32

own experience. My blindness was caused by an automobile accident — the boy driving the other vehicle was drunk."

He said it calmly and matter-of-factly, obviously expecting no response. "I suppose I should warn you, Jennifer," he continued with a smile, "that you would probably have to put in quite a few weekends and evenings. But I'd make it up to you. You could have time off through the week every now and then. By the way, do you like to jock? Would you want a show of your own?"

"Actually, that's one of my favorite parts of the business," Jennifer admitted quickly, growing more and more interested in the job.

"Well, you could have your choice right now between two shows. I need someone for a live talk show in the evening, or you could have a three-hour drive in the afternoon."

Jennifer was hooked. "I think I'd really like the job, Mr. Kaine."

"The name's *Dan*, OK? You've got a dynamite voice, Jennifer, you know that? Should be great on the air."

Before she could reply, Kaine went on in his slow, soothing drawl. "Can I ask you about something else? Gabe filled me in on most of your background, but I've got to admit that I'm curious about how you went from studying opera in Rome to a radio station in West Virginia."

Jennifer was deliberately evasive, hoping he wouldn't press her for details. "I — well, it's kind of a long story."

"That's all right," Kaine said agreeably, as if he had all the time in the world.

Jennifer swallowed with difficulty, feeling her stomach knot with tension. The memories were still painful — too painful to discuss with a stranger, even one who seemed as kind as Daniel Kaine. "Mr. Kaine — Dan — I don't think it's relevant. And it is . . . personal."

He looked surprised but recovered quickly. Obviously, he had no intention of retreating from the subject. "Your sheet said you'd studied voice for a long time. Two years in Rome with some famous *maestro*, right? Then you came home, went to O.U. for a degree in communications, and worked in a radio station on the side." He paused, but only for an instant. "You were interested in a stage career in opera?"

"I . . . was at one time, yes."

"Why did you change directions?"

After a noticeable hesitation, Jennifer answered quietly, her tone flat and unemotional. "Because I wasn't good enough to do

34

what I had originally hoped to do."

Kaine tapped his long, blunt fingers lightly on the desk. "Who said?"

Jennifer made a weak attempt at lightness. "One of the best voice coaches in Europe. He said it very kindly, of course."

Picking up a pencil, he twirled it back and forth between the thumb and two fingers of one hand. "That's rough. Is that what you had always wanted, to have an operatic career?"

Jennifer blinked furiously against the hot wetness burning her eyes. Impatient with herself and unsettled by his apparent determination to press the issue, she remained silent, even though he was obviously waiting for some sort of reply from her.

After an awkward silence, he went on. "The pain's still pretty fresh, is it, Jennifer?" he questioned softly.

If she admitted the truth she would feel foolish. It sounded so petty in contrast to the enormity of Daniel Kaine's problem. Her own loss suddenly seemed pathetically insignificant as she studied him. She wondered at his air of self-assurance, his apparent tranquility. It had to be a front, she told herself defensively. No one with that kind of disability could possibly be as emotionally . . . *together* as he appeared to be. No, she concluded abruptly, either this man was some sort of a rare spiritual giant or he had simply erected one of the most impressive facades she had ever encountered. Her instincts suspected the latter. At any rate, she felt a grudging touch of respect for him.

Once more Kaine met her silence with the same easygoing, pleasant tone of voice. "So this job is what? An alternative?"

"Yes," Jennifer replied tersely. "An alternative."

To her surprise, he smiled. "You want it just for the money?"

Jennifer had always found it impossible to be less than honest. "That's the biggest reason, yes. My father mortgaged almost everything we have to send me to Italy. I have two younger brothers, one who just got married and another . . . in a private school. It's time I paid my own way."

"I can understand that," Kaine said agreeably, still smiling. "What about moving? Would that present a problem for you?"

So he hadn't written her off after all! "No, it wouldn't," Jennifer said immediately. "My only ties are my family — and I wouldn't be all that far away from them. And, Mr. Kaine — *Dan* — what I said about the job being an alternative . . . I'd still do my best for you, I honestly would."

His smile grew even warmer, and his voice held a note of interest when he spoke again. "You're not intimidated by me — by my blindness — are you?"

"I —" She stopped, considering his question. "No. No, I don't think I am."

With one last tap of his fingers on the desk, he rose from his chair and walked slowly around to her, extending his hand. "I thought not. Well, we need to see about finding an apartment for you. Will you need a furnished or unfurnished place?"

He was offering her the job! Just like that. Jennifer stood up, shook his hand, and smiled brightly. "Furnished. And cheap," she added.

Kaine grinned. "We'll get Gabe and my sister, Lyss, to help us with that. Lyss is coming over to go to lunch with us in a while; we can talk to her about it then. How soon do you think you could start, once we find you a place to live?"

"Two weeks?"

"Great. I'll call Gabe in a minute and see if Lyss is here yet."

For an instant, he appeared to consider something. Then, his expression briefly uncertain, he dipped his head down. "Jennifer?" His voice was soft and halting. "I wonder — would you mind if I . . . looked at you? With my hands?"

Something caught and tightened in Jennifer's throat, but she ignored it. "No — I mean, I don't mind at all."

It was an unsettling experience. She hadn't expected such gentleness, not from such a big man. He rested his hands lightly on her shoulders for just an instant before moving to trace the oval of her face, hesitantly at first, then with more confidence. He molded her face between his large hands, shaping every feature with light but firm strokes.

"You're tall. What . . . five-seven?"

"Eight," Jennifer said tightly, clearing her throat. "Five-eight, actually."

Kaine nodded and smiled thoughtfully. "That's good. Short women make me a little crazy. I never seem to be able to find them, you know? Never know how far down they are."

Jennifer stared blankly into his face, then laughed, but only for a moment. So unexpectedly intense was her response to his touch that she had to close her eyes against it. His fingertips were heavily calloused, and she fleetingly wondered what sort of work a blind man might do to cause calluses. His hands explored slowly, brushing over her high forehead, lightly winging out from her eyes, barely touching her closed eyelids, seeming to take note of her eyelashes before moving down over her cheekbones and the hollows beneath. He allowed his thumbs to touch the outside corners of her mouth only briefly, but long enough for her to catch a sharp, uneven breath before he fanned his fingertips gently along her jawline.

"I don't think you eat very much, Jennifer," he said softly, smiling as though he had discovered a small secret.

"My youngest brother calls me Bones, if that tells you anything," Jennifer volunteered. Her voice sounded terribly unnatural. She thought she would choke when he touched the dimple in the middle of her chin, then slid his hands slowly outward to scan the length of her hair. He murmured something she didn't catch, then asked, "What color is your hair?"

"Uh . . . it's dark brown. With some red — auburn, I guess you'd call it." She hoped he wouldn't detect the slight tremor in her voice.

"Must take forever to dry," he commented with a small, thoughtful smile. He moved one finger back to the scar just in front of her right ear. "What happened here?"

Jennifer could hardly believe the sensitivity of his hands. That scar was barely noticeable, even to her. "I fell off a horse at a girlfriend's farm when I was twelve. A piece of barbed-wire fence got in my way."

"Tomboy, huh?" he chuckled softly.

"I'm afraid so." She wondered if the jelly sensation in her knees was due to lack of sleep or his touch.

His hands quickly framed her face once more, very gently, then dropped away. "Thank you, Jennifer, for understanding my need to do that." His features softened even more. "Gabe told me you were lovely," he said quietly, with a nod of agreement. Then he grinned. "*Bones*, huh? Sounds like something I'd say to *my* sister."

Though she was trim and fit, the name "Bones" hardly described Alyssa Kaine. A physical education teacher at the Christian school that she, Dan, and Gabe Denton had once attended, Lyss had the same athletic build as her brother. As the four of them laughed and talked over lunch at a nearby restaurant, Jennifer knew she had already made her first friends in Shepherd Valley.

"Papa Joe" Como, the proprietor of the restaurant, also owned some rental property in town. As soon as he learned that Jennifer was going to be working at the radio station, he insisted on showing her a house that would be "perfect" for her use.

40

Jennifer fell in love with the quaint three-room bungalow and its white wicker furniture almost immediately. And "Papa Joe," who seemed far more interested in finding a tenant who would take care of his property than in charging an exorbitant rent, quoted a monthly rate well within her reach. They finalized the arrangement with a down payment and a handshake.

When she was finally ready to leave, Dan walked her to her car, accompanied by Sunny. After she was settled behind the steering wheel, he leaned down to her window. Jennifer again had the disturbing sensation that he was looking directly into her eyes.

"Well . . . hurry back, Jennifer," he said softly in a tone that sounded almost wistful. He touched her shoulder lightly, then straightened. "We'll have a welcome party for you once you get settled."

Jennifer watched him from her rearview mirror for as long as possible — this tall, dark, enigma of a man with his golden companion standing quietly at his side. For the first time in years, she felt a trace of hopeful anticipation. She was surprised to realize that she wanted the next two weeks to pass quickly. *Very* quickly.

41

THREE

Dan pulled a fisherman's sweater over his head as he walked into the kitchen. Suddenly, he stopped and stood listening, his hands in the back pockets of his jeans.

He heard nothing, but for the first time in almost five years, he was engulfed by the same blood-chilling sensation that had plagued him during the early months of his blindness. That oppressive, menacing feeling that he was being watched — like a bug under glass. Isolated. Vulnerable. Helpless.

Perspiration started on the palms of his hands, and he felt the beginning of a tremor in his arms and legs. His heart pumped harder, and he braced one hand on the counter to steady himself. He tried to swallow but couldn't. All he could do was wait until it passed.

The rehabilitation counselor in Pittsburgh had warned him that he could expect occasional anxiety attacks indefinitely, but he had hoped that was all behind him. *It's these crazy phone calls,* he told himself. They were coming nearly every night now, and sometimes through the day at the station. Rarely did the man say anything; usually the line remained ominously silent. Last night the

42

phone had rung long after midnight. When Dan answered, he heard nothing but the sound of ragged breathing.

He caught his breath now, aware that his heartbeat was gradually leveling off. Feeling weak, he wiped his hands on his jeans and lowered himself to one of the stools at the counter to wait for his head to clear.

He knew he should tell someone about the calls. But he also knew what it would mean if he did. Everyone would start hovering over him again, watching him, *protecting* him. His mother. Gabe. Lyss. Even his dad. It would be like before, during the weeks following the accident. He would lose his freedom, his independence again.

No way. Not yet. He would say nothing until he absolutely had to.

What good would it do anyway? What could he tell them? That some crazy man seemed bent on driving him over the edge? Even though he had sensed the sick anger and something akin to hatred behind the voice on the phone, the man had made no real threat.

So far.

The dream was coming more often now, too. It was different — more demanding, more harrowing than ever before. There was nothing he could do to prevent it. His subconscious seemed to have a will of its own, though he'd tried everything he could think of to avoid a repeat of the nightmare. It was always the same.

He would sleep uneasily, a sleep with no real peace, then would suddenly find himself on that same winding mountain road again. He would hang the corkscrew curve near the top of the hill only to be met by two blazing halos of light looming toward him through the fog. He would feel himself suspended, weightless, for a brief spark of eternity. Then the mushrooming headlights of the oncoming truck, like two furious, malevolent eyes, would explode into his face. Terror would grip him by the throat as metal rammed metal, while glass shattered and blew to pieces in a slow-motion kaleidoscope of horror.

And then he would hear someone scream, not realizing it was his own voice until the smoking chamber of the car echoed the sound of it over and over again before tossing it out into the night. Finally, he would gape through shock-glazed eyes at the last thing he would ever see in his lifetime — a face behind the windshield of the truck, a face fragmented and distorted by broken glass and a heavy shroud of mist. The face of fear, a macabre rictus, frozen in an endless, silent scream . . .

And then the nightmare would end. Always at the same point, always in the same way, always incomplete. He would awaken, at first in a storm of panic, then weary and drained with the reality that it was only a dream, that it was over . . . but that he was, indeed, blind. He would lie quietly, sweating, trembling, forcing himself to think about the dream — for there was always something unfinished about it, something he could never quite remember.

He supposed the telephone calls could somehow be triggering the old anxieties. He wondered, too, if the calls might possibly be connected to the upcoming radiothon. The station had recently begun to highlight the nationwide campaign with hourly announcements, many by Dan himself. It wouldn't be the first time someone who was already a little unhinged went off the deep end because he didn't like what he heard on the air.

With a resigned sigh, Dan straightened his shoulders and hauled himself to his feet. This was *not* the best frame of mind for the coming evening. He forced himself to shake off the melancholy that had threatened to engulf his emotions most of the day, like a low-hanging cloud that refused to move.

Jennifer — and half the town, he reminded himself wryly — would be here within minutes. *Jennifer.* He said her name to himself, quietly, with a touch of a smile, relishing the sound of it on his lips. *I'm in trouble, all right. But maybe not the kind I've been worried about. The real trouble, I suspect, has a lot more to do with a certain lady who always smells like a vanilla-scented candle and has a voice like warm, thick honey. The same lady who, according to Gabe, has exactly four freckles on her nose and looks like a model for an aerobics advertisement.*

The lady also happened to be the guest of honor at the party he would be hosting in a few minutes.

Dan tried to shove his attention back to more mundane matters, but the thought of Jennifer's presence in his home — an entire evening to simply be close to her, to hear that sensational laugh of hers, to fill his senses with the sunshine-warm fragrance of her hair at his shoulder — made his smile break even wider across his face. He tried to push aside his own adolescent foolishness, but the glow of his smile lingered.

With a self-mocking shrug, he pursed his lips in a soft whistle, palmed a few pretzels from a bowl on the snack-heaped harvest table in the dining area, and walked into the living room. He stopped in front of the fire-place, where flames were rising and crackling cheerfully.

Sunny padded in and lay down at his side. Dan stooped down and began to stroke the golden retriever. He knew her favorite rubber ducky was resting snugly between her two front paws. After feeding her a pretzel from his hand, he muttered a reminder to himself that "you must never spoil a guide dog, Mr. Kaine." *Absolutely.*

He stood, flexed his shoulders, and began to pace the length of the room. In truth, it was an unbroken flow of rooms with no walls, furnished with primitive accent pieces and early West Virginia carpentry. When he reached the "music room" at the far end of the first floor, he stopped to insert a CD into a player on the bookcase shelf. Jerking the volume control well past the comfort level, he shoved his hands into his pockets and breaking into a satisfied smile, began to sing along with a contemporary Christian band.

Sunny reluctantly stirred. Dan could imagine the retriever turning a long-suffering, mildly censuring look at him, as though to make the observation that he was becoming more and more peculiar lately.

Jennifer changed clothes for the third time

and took a long, disgruntled look at herself in the mirror. "What is *wrong* with me tonight?" she muttered to herself. "You'd think I had a date at the governor's mansion."

Rummaging through several boxes, she found the leather boots she had bought on sale the winter before and hurriedly pulled them on. She frowned at herself again in the full-length mirror on the bedroom door, deciding too late that the casual slacks and oversized jacket made her look even thinner than she was. She buttoned one large button, considered the effect, then immediately unbuttoned it. She had skipped too many meals during the hectic days of packing and moving, and it showed.

She raked a brush through her hair, then paused, her hand suspended above her head, as she realized that the one person she was so anxious to impress couldn't even see the result of her efforts!

"Brilliant, Jennifer," she said under her breath, grabbing her shoulder bag and slinging it over her arm. "Absolutely brilliant."

She shrugged quickly into her coat and began to fish for her car keys as she raced out the door. Tripping on the front step, she choked with exasperation when she dropped her purse upside down, spilling its contents all over the small cement porch. She scrambled to pick up the clutter, shoving a collection of eight or nine pens and pencils back to the bottom of the bag, along with her wallet, her pocket organizer, half a dozen stamps, two Hershey bars — but no keys.

Fuming, she walked into the carport. A quick glance through the window of the Honda confirmed that the keys were still in the ignition. She tried the door and discovered with relief that she hadn't locked it.

She had to stop living this way. She had to get organized, take control of her life. She really did.

She drove with extreme caution, deliberately holding in check what her dad called her "lead foot." The streets were little more than mounds of drifted snow and thin layers of ice. The road crews apparently hadn't been able to keep up with the fast-falling, wind-driven snow that had begun in the afternoon, even though it seemed to have finally stopped.

In spite of some faint apprehension about meeting so many new people all at once — the list Dan's secretary had shown her earlier in the week looked as though most of Shepherd Valley would be there tonight — she was looking forward to the evening. She was curious about the way Dan lived and was eager to see his home. At first she had been surprised to learn that he lived alone and wondered how he could manage, even with Sunny to help. But after three weeks of daily contact with the man, she no longer questioned Daniel Kaine's ability to manage anything.

The light she had been waiting for changed, and Jennifer moved through the intersection slowly, her mind still filled with thoughts of her enigmatic boss. There was no denying the attraction the man held for her, though she had scolded herself more than once for allowing him to occupy such a prominent place among her thoughts. Still, he was an intriguing, complex personality, far different from anyone Jennifer had ever known. As for the way her emotions ran riot every time he came near — well, he was simply a very *compelling* man.

He was also a strangely *intimate* man. This trait might have put her off in someone without Dan's innate kindness and acute sensitivity. But Jennifer had quickly grown comfortable with his eagerness to know, to understand, to "see" through the eyes of others what he could no longer see for himself.

It was now routine for her to give him at least a sketchy idea of what she was wearing, especially color, or to casually describe their surroundings when they were driving. She told him of any significant change in another employee's appearance and fell into the habit of describing little things that caught her attention whenever they were together.

She had come to understand that he drew heavily upon his memories and considered himself fortunate in having been sighted most of his life. He was still able to project images onto the screen of his mind, he had explained to her, whereas those who had been blind from birth had to depend upon the observations of someone else, plus whatever they could glean from their other senses, to help them form mental pictures.

Jennifer hadn't said anything, but she was more than a little skeptical about his positive attitude. She found it almost impossible to see even the smallest grain of "blessing" in the tragedy of Dan's blindness. So far, however, she had seen no trace of anything that might hint of false courage or shallow optimism.

It would be difficult *not* to be drawn to the man, she assured herself once more as she turned slowly onto Keystone Drive. In addition to his commanding physical presence and multifaceted personality, he bore his disability with an incredible aplomb. Dan obviously relished his independence, yet he didn't hesitate to ask for assistance when he needed it. There was a definite aura of strength about him, even though a touching vulnerability would occasionally surface when least expected, as had been the case earlier in the afternoon. Jennifer had walked into Dan's office and found him standing at the large window behind his desk, his face and one hand pressed to the glass as though he were staring outside. As usual, his dark hair had fallen over his forehead, barely brushing the pale vertical scar at his eyebrow. He had been dressed in a white crewneck pullover with a quilted front and gray cotton trousers with worn knees. He wore the casual outfit as he wore everything else — with the natural grace of an athlete comfortable with his own body. But there had been a sadness imprinted on his features that tugged at Jennifer's heart. She had felt a sudden intense need to say or do something that would bring a smile to his face.

She hadn't spoken, feeling awkward about intruding upon what was obviously an unprotected, private moment. But he had known she was there.

"Jennifer?" he questioned softly, without moving.

"Yes. I can come back —"

"No, it's all right," he assured her quickly, motioning her closer. "Come in."

She went to stand by him, seeing the vapor his warm breath had made on the cold windowpane.

"Katharine said it was snowing," he said quietly.

"Yes, it is. It started about an hour ago."

He rubbed his fingers gently against the glass, as though he could touch the scene outside. "I used to love to stand here and look down on the valley when it was snowing." His expression was pensive. "Do you like it — the snow?"

"Oh, yes. I love it! I always have."

He was quiet for a moment. Then he touched her lightly on the shoulder. "Help me see it again, Jennifer. Tell me what it looks like."

The wistful note in his appeal had thrown Jennifer off guard for just an instant. She glanced from Dan's profile to the winter scene outside, forcing her voice into an even, conversational tone when she spoke.

"Well, let's see . . . it's dark, almost like evening. The street lights are on all the way down the hill — lots of houses are lit up, too. And most of the cars have their headlights on. It looks as if traffic's having a hard time already. I can see at least four or five

53

cars stalled halfway up Rainbow Drive."

She stopped, moving closer to him to peer out the window. "It's a heavy snow. The branches on that old blue spruce by the walk are really drooping." Then she added, as much to herself as to Dan, "The snowflakes are the big, fat squishy ones, the kind that are fun to catch with your mouth open."

She looked up at him. The melancholy that had darkened his features only moments before had now lifted and brightened to a tender smile of remembrance. When he reached for her, fumbling to find her hand, Jennifer linked her fingers with his without thinking.

"Did your mom ever yell at you for messing up her window like this?" Dan asked. He blew against the window, then took her hand and pressed her index finger against the cold, wet glass. *J-e-n-n-i-f-e-r.*"

"My turn." Still smiling, he transferred his hand from on top of hers to trace his finger in the fog on the glass.

"Wait a minute — we ran out of steam," Jennifer told him, laughing. "Breathe."

"I am breathing."

"On the *window,* Dan. We need more steam."

"Right. More steam." He opened his mouth to blow on the glass, then stopped.

"Ah . . . tell me there's no one else in the room, Jennifer."

"Just us."

He leaned his forehead lightly against the glass, quickly steaming up more of the window, and Jennifer helped him write his name beneath hers.

"This is a very symbolic thing we've done here today, Jennifer," he said gravely. "You realize that, don't you?"

"Symbolic?"

"Absolutely." He dabbed his wet, cold finger on the end of her nose. "Once you write your name in a man's breath, you become a part of his life."

Even now, remembering the moment set Jennifer's heart racing. She had better get a grip, and soon. *He wasn't serious,* she reminded herself. *It was a joke. Nothing more.*

Jennifer forced her thoughts back to the present as she killed the motor of the car. Leaning back with a relieved sigh, she studied the "Kaine barn," Dan's home. She had already heard a great deal about it. It was as unconventional and as unique as its owner. It truly *was* a barn — a large, restored early American barn attached to a small clapboard house, which, as Dan had explained to her, now housed his indoor pool. Structurally spectacular, it had a sturdy, rustic appearance — dark oak siding, seamed metal roof, and varied styles and sizes of windows. It was tucked into the hillside and looked down on an absolutely breathtaking view of the valley.

She dragged in a deep, steadying sigh as she slid out from under the steering wheel and began to trudge up the snow-covered walk to the house. "Speaking of breathtaking views," she muttered softly to herself.

She stopped to stare for a long moment at Daniel Kaine, who had just thrown open the door and stood waiting for her with a smile that made her heart go into an unexpected tailspin.

FOUR

Dan dropped his hands lightly onto Jennifer's shoulders as he helped her shrug out of her coat. "Relax, kid. Mountaineers are very friendly folks. You don't need to get tensed up about being in a room full of them."

Jennifer shook her head, marveling at his uncanny ability to sense her emotional barometer. "Nobody's ever given a party for me before. I'm a little nervous."

He squeezed her shoulders reassuringly and was just turning to hang up her coat when Lyss walked up and took it from him. Jennifer stared at the two of them together, Lyss and Dan, struck again by how much they resembled each other. Lyss was as striking in her own way as Dan, with the same penetrating blue eyes and dusky hair that appeared to be trademarks of the Kaines.

Naturally, it wasn't long before Gabe joined them. Jennifer had observed that wherever Lyss was, Gabe was sure to follow. The two were engaged — and had been, Dan had informed her, for nearly two years. Apparently Lyss was the holdout, insisting they have a down payment for a house before they married.

The four of them started toward the kitchen, only to be stopped on the way by a small boy with silver-blond hair and apple cheeks. He came bounding up, with Sunny at his heels. Dan grinned tolerantly and hoisted the boy up to his shoulder in one easy motion. "Did you and Jim give Sunny her dinner like I asked?"

"We put some good stuff in with her dog food, Dan. Hamburger and eggs." The boy gave Dan a hug and Jennifer a bashful smile.

Jennifer grinned at him. She had already met Jason Lyle at church. The small eight-year-old with the enormous brown eyes was an orphan — mentally limited, but only slightly — who lived at the county children's home. Both of his parents had been killed in a motorcycle accident when he was only a few months old. Dan had first become acquainted with the boy through the Friend-to-Friend Association, a countywide mutual aid ministry for the disabled that Dan and some of the people at his church had helped to establish. The Kaines and Gabe took turns seeing that Jason got to church and Sunday school each week.

He was an incredibly beautiful child, Jennifer thought, so physically perfect that it was difficult to realize he might never exceed the mental capacity he had already attained.

She couldn't be near the boy without feeling a stab of resentment at the cruel blow that had been dealt to him. How could God give a child such remarkable appeal and then cripple his mind?

Jason never failed to remind her of her younger brother Loren — gifted with an unusually fine mind but an imperfect body. To Jennifer's thinking, Loren and Jason were only two among many examples of divine injustice.

She watched Dan swing the boy over his head and then set him lightly on his feet. There was an obvious flow of affection between the two of them. It was no secret around the station that Dan would like to adopt his little friend but was reluctant to do so because he wanted more for Jason than what he thought he could offer as a blind, single parent.

"Go get Jim and the two of you take Sunny outside for a few minutes," Dan instructed Jason. "And bundle up good, you hear?"

Jennifer watched the small boy trot off to the kitchen and begin to tug eagerly on Jim Arbegunst's sleeve. Jim, the tall, sad-eyed teenager she had first seen in the studio on the day of her interview, was helping Papa Joe with the food. Jennifer had been immediately drawn to this boy with his uncertain smile and haunted eyes. He worked part-time at the station after school and on weekends. Gabe often referred to Jim, who followed Dan around with undisguised devotion, as "another one of Kaine's kids."

A quiet, noticeably unhappy youth, Jim was the only son of a farmer who lived on a small plot of land just outside of town — a piece of ground Dan described as too anemic to yield anything more than a token crop of vegetables. According to Dan, Caleb Arbegunst supplemented his income by running a temporary shelter for delinquent boys, a kind of stopping-off place where the court sent youngsters until more permanent arrangements could be made.

Apparently, some residents of the community had mixed emotions about the shelter. From time to time, questions were raised about the advisability of placing so many teens in the care of a man with Arbegunst's reputation. He was rumored to be an alcoholic with a fiery temper, and some believed that his wife, who had deserted Caleb and Jim when the boy was still a toddler, had left because she could no longer deal with her husband's cruelty.

Dan's voice pulled Jennifer's attention back to him. "My folks sent their best wishes — and their regrets that they couldn't be here." He moved Jennifer's hand to his forearm and covered it with his own as they began to walk through the house. "They won't be back from the convention until late tomorrow night. But they want you to come to lunch Sunday after church."

Jennifer had already been to the Kaines' twice for dinner and would have jumped at any invitation to enjoy Pauline Kaine's cooking again. "You're sure I won't wear out my welcome?"

"No chance. However, I *do* have an ulterior motive for getting you invited."

"Oh?"

"Mm-hm. I was wondering if you'd be willing to drive me up to the farm afterward. I should warn you, I suppose, that I'd like to take Jason along, too." He stopped walking and turned toward her.

"The farm?" Jennifer was distracted by the music room at the far end of the house. Her glance traveled over an ebony grand piano occupying an enormous amount of space, two sophisticated-looking keyboards, a drum set, and a number of smaller stringed instruments. On either side, tall bookshelves held an impressive stereo component system.

"Helping Hand," Dan went on. "The summer camp for disabled kids I told you about." Located about sixty miles from

Shepherd Valley, the Helping Hand had once been a conventional farm. For the last three years, Dan and Gabe had been working hard to turn it into a large camp that could accommodate children with a variety of physical and emotional challenges.

"Oh — sure, I can go. No problem." Jennifer expelled a quick breath of surprise. "You never told me you were a musician!"

He gave a deprecating shrug. "I just play around with the keyboards some. It relaxes me. Mostly I use all this with my teen group. I like to have them out here to practice instead of rehearsing in the church basement. You'd be surprised at the cooperation I get when I promise a swimming party in exchange for a good rehearsal."

"I've heard a lot about your teen choir. How big is it?"

He grinned. "Don't ever let them hear you call them a *choir*, Jennifer. They're an *ensemble*, or a *group*, or even a *bunch* — but never, ever a *choir*. We usually have about fifteen. Ask me on a bad night, and I'd say fifty."

"And he loves every minute of it," added Lyss, who, along with Gabe, had followed them from the great room. "He and his drummer."

"His drummer?"

"In person," Gabe said, poking his head

over Lyss's shoulder. "The kids call me *Sticks*."

"That's for your legs, man, not your drumming," Dan cracked.

"Uh, huh . . . well, you don't want to know what they call you, old buddy," Gabe retorted dryly.

The three of them insisted on showing Jennifer the pool house, Dan's special pride and joy. By the time they returned to the main living area, the house was filled with guests milling about.

Jennifer spent the next half hour meeting people, then went upstairs to the loft with Lyss and Jason. The boy had had an accident with his fruit punch and was in need of a quick cleanup.

"This is where I sleep when I spend the night with Dan. I even keep some of my clothes here," Jason told her proudly as they entered the large bedroom.

For an instant, Jennifer had the peculiar sensation that she had just stepped onto a nineteenth-century ship. The room held a variety of nautical items, including a splendid teak-and-brass binnacle and a hand-rubbed ship's wheel. The massive bureau was topped by a model of a clipper ship, and the wall shelves were lined with such artifacts as a whaling harpoon, different kinds of lanterns, an antique compass, and a bell clock. The only things not directly related to the sea were the huge half-tester bed, covered with a colorful quilt, and a stone fireplace with an old, broad-bottom rocking chair in front of it.

Jennifer breathed a long, appreciative sigh. "What a *wonderful* room! Dan must love the sea!"

Lyss nodded as she scooped a clean shirt from a bureau drawer and helped Jason change. "He does. He and Gabe were always building ship models when they were kids. Before the accident, they used to run white water on the Cheat River every chance they got. Dan has always been crazy about water — anything from the ocean to a swimming pool." With a smile, she gave Jason an affectionate swat on the bottom and sent him on his way. The boy flashed Jennifer a mischievous grin as he raced by her and headed for the steps.

"The loft used to be just one big room," Lyss explained, gesturing to an open doorway opposite the bureau. "But Dan started doing so much counseling a couple of years ago that we partitioned off enough space to make a guest room for visitors."

"Counseling?"

Lyss took a moment to run a comb

through her dark hair, glancing over her shoulder in the mirror at Jennifer. "Every now and then one of the therapists from the rehab center in Pittsburgh sends someone down here to stay a few days, someone who's having a hard time emotionally."

"I don't know how he does it," Jennifer said, shaking her head. "How does he keep up with everything? He must never have a moment for himself!"

"Well, he likes to keep busy. Sometimes I think he takes on a little too much, but —" She shrugged, leaving the thought incomplete.

"Lyss — how long did it take? For Dan to get over the accident?"

Lyss turned, pushed up the sleeves of her bright red sweater, and walked to a nearby window, glancing out for a moment. When she turned back to Jennifer, her expression was grave. "I'm not sure anyone ever really gets over something like that."

Feeling rebuked, Jennifer nodded. "It's just that he's so . . ." She groped for a word, finding none.

"I know." Lyss smiled a little and went to sit down on the bed, motioning for Jennifer to do the same. "It was difficult — horribly difficult — for a long time. Sometimes I didn't think he would ever be himself again," she said quietly. For a moment her attention seemed to drift away, and she sat plucking idly at the bed quilt.

"It's hard to imagine Dan ever being different than he is now," Jennifer said. "He has to be the most amazing man I've ever met."

Still not looking up, Lyss nodded and continued to smile. "He's pretty terrific." She ran her hand through her short, casually styled hair, then glanced across the bed at Jennifer. "He was such a great athlete. Did you know he took a gold at the Olympics? He's a marvelous swimmer! Of course, he's always excelled at anything he attempted —"

She stopped short and laughed. "Listen to me — I'm sorry. I'm afraid I'm not always very humble where my big brother is concerned."

"No, I understand," Jennifer protested. "You have every right to be proud of him."

"I *am* proud of him. I think he's wonderful," Lyss declared almost fiercely. "It was a nightmare, seeing him lose so much, watching him fight so desperately to hold on to his dignity — and his sanity. He had to start all over again, just like a child —" Her bright blue eyes glistened with unshed tears, and Jennifer impulsively reached across the bed to squeeze her hand with understanding.

"That's what was hardest for me," Lyss explained in a quieter voice. "Seeing him so . . . defeated, so helpless. Dan's always been my hero. With six years between us, he spoiled me terribly the whole time I was growing up."

She was obviously remembering things she would rather forget. "It was *awful*, seeing him like that, reduced to almost total help-lessness. Watching him trip, bump into walls, stumble, having to stand by while he tried to feed himself without spilling —" She stopped, her voice again shaky. But after a moment her expression cleared, and she went on. "Of course, that was all before his rehabilitation, and Sunny. After he came back from Seeing Eye, he hired a therapist to give him special mobility training. It was amazing to see what Dan learned in such a short time — how to arrange his clothing, code his money, organize the kitchen. The therapist even gave him a crash course in self-defense."

Lyss got to her feet and walked around the bed toward Jennifer, who also stood. "Without a doubt, Dan's determination to be independent is one of the things that kept him going after the accident." She attempted a smile. "Of course, that unbearable stub-bornness of his may have been a factor, too.

But over the long haul, it had to be his faith in God that helped him survive."

Jennifer's reply was faint. "I wonder how he did it." She glanced at Lyss. "How he managed to . . . go on trusting, under the circumstances?"

Lyss studied Jennifer, her gaze questioning but patient. "I don't think anyone but Dan could explain that," she answered.

"Can I ask you one more thing — about the accident? What actually happened?"

"Oh, I thought maybe Gabe had told you, or even Dan. He'll talk about it, you know; you don't have to avoid the subject with him. Actually, what made the whole thing even worse for me was that Dan was on his way back from visiting me at the university the night it happened."

Her face contorted briefly with the pain of remembrance. "It was my birthday, but I had finals and couldn't come home. So Dan drove down to deliver my birthday presents. He did that a lot," she said, smiling a little as she continued. "He would just show up, without warning, always bringing me something — a new book or clothes or money." Her voice softened. "He was forever bringing me money. I always seemed to be broke when I was in college."

"And the accident happened on his way

home?" Jennifer prompted gently.

Lyss nodded, leaning wearily against the doorframe. "It was late, and there was a heavy fog. It was a head-on collision."

"The other driver — he was killed, wasn't he?"

Again Lyss's eyes misted. "Yes. He was only sixteen. Apparently he was drunk — at least he'd been drinking a lot. The state police told us they found an empty bottle at his feet, and his clothes reeked of liquor. They said the boy had probably died instantly from a broken neck, even though Caleb ran for help as soon as he was able."

"Caleb?"

"Caleb Arbegunst. Jim's father. You see, it was his truck. The boy who was driving was one of the boys from the shelter. Caleb was taking him to the detention center, but he got sleepy and let the boy drive. Evidently he started drinking as soon as Caleb fell asleep. Caleb didn't know the boy had alcohol with him."

Lyss's mouth twisted with disgust. "At least he *said* he didn't know. For my part, I don't believe much of anything Caleb Arbegunst says."

"You know, I don't think I've heard a good word about that man since I came to Shepherd Valley," Jennifer said.

"And it's not likely that you will, because no one can find anything good to say," Lyss told her, still frowning. "Anyway, Caleb was thrown from the truck and was unconscious for a long time. When he came to, he went to a nearby farmhouse to call the state police. They found the boy dead and Dan unconscious."

An involuntary shudder gripped Jennifer for an instant. "And when Dan woke up . . ."

"He was blind."

They were both silent for a long moment. Finally, Lyss gave a long sigh, then smiled. "Let's get you back downstairs. You're supposed to be the guest of honor at this shindig, remember?"

Later in the evening, about the time Jennifer would have expected the party to break up, people began urging Dan and Gabe down to the music room. Lyss went along, making her way to one of the keyboards while Gabe sat down at the drums.

Jennifer watched the three with delighted surprise, her mouth dropping open when Dan crashed into a thunderous cadence at the piano, then unexpectedly broke away to the driving beat of a top Christian contemporary number. Gabe immediately backed him up on the drums, and after the first few measures Lyss added the keyboard — and her voice. She and Dan blended together in a tight, professional harmony. Almost instantly, everyone in the room became a part of the music, clapping their hands or singing along through a number of contemporary and traditional gospel songs.

Jennifer continued to gape with amazement at Dan. So he "played around with the keyboards some," huh? A warmth enveloped her heart as she watched him. He could probably do anything he wanted at a keyboard, she speculated, and his voice was more than adequate. The man never seemed to run out of surprises!

The noise level in the room skyrocketed as Gabe plopped a green baseball cap onto Dan's head and strapped an old flattop guitar around his neck. When Gabe reached back into the corner for a fiddle for himself, Lyss picked up a banjo — and everyone went crazy.

For the next twenty minutes, the trio indulged themselves in a bluegrass demonstration that left Jennifer wide-eyed and openmouthed. She was astonished at the way Gabe could grind the fiddle, even more fascinated by Dan and his guitar as he turned it from a mournful, whining freight train one minute into a flashy, frenzied blaze of superior "pickin'" the next. Now she knew why his fingertips were so calloused.

At one point, she was caught short by an unexpected — and unwelcome — pang of yearning. "This group could use a singer with a little class," Gabe jokingly called out to her. For one precarious moment Jennifer was tempted.

It had been a long, difficult road, burying the desire to sing, a desire that at one time had been more powerful for Jennifer than the craving for food. But bury it she had. Or so she had thought. Now here it was again, that aching, all-too-familiar pulsing in her veins that cried for an outlet. The need to create, to communicate, to celebrate —

No! With a determination that bordered on anger, she slammed the door of her mind, shook her head at Gabe, and forced her attention back to the music. The three of them continued to ham it up to the hilt until Lyss gave up her banjo in defeat, collapsing in a fit of laughter at the slapstick antics of Gabe and her brother. Finally, Dan tipped his baseball cap to the crowd, then tossed his arm around Gabe's shoulder.

Jennifer stared at Dan, once again puzzling over his apparent enjoyment of life. Not for the first time, she wondered if the peace that seemed to emanate from him could actually be genuine. She found it increasingly difficult to doubt what she saw in him, yet in some inexplicable way Dan's strength and contentment stirred a sense of uneasiness in her own spirit that she found herself unwilling to face — as well as a longing that bordered on envy, envy for whatever it was that gave his life such a unique, shining quality.

For Dan was a man who lived his life in darkness — or, as he had once corrected her, in "grayness." Because of his blindness, he walked among shadows, his steps guided only by his own personal faith. Yet he managed to shed a gentle, steady light on his surroundings wherever he went.

Was it possible that she even *resented* his boundless passion for living, his inconceivable serenity and strength? Perhaps his strength evoked in her some nameless guilt for her own lack of spiritual maturity. The very idea made Jennifer wonder what kind of person she had become.

Almost irritably, she also wondered why she should be spending so much time and energy thinking of Dan at all.

But that was another question for which she had no answer.

The truck was well hidden in the thick

grove of pine trees at the side of Kaine's house. He had parked just high enough on the first rise of the hill so he could watch without being seen.

He could see everyone leaving now, laughing, calling back and forth to one another as they half walked and half slid to their cars. He had been waiting for over two hours. It hadn't been so bad at first. As long as everyone was inside, he could run the engine and keep the heater going. But when they started coming out, he was afraid someone would hear the truck, so he'd killed the motor. Now he was shaking with the cold. He crossed his arms over his chest and hugged them to his body as tightly as he could, shivering even as his anger heated.

Kaine must have had half the town in there. You wouldn't think a blind man would be throwing parties. But Kaine wanted everybody to think he was no different from anyone else.

Like the way he'd come on to the woman. He had seen the two of them before tonight, smiling at each other, just as though they were a normal couple, like they belonged together. Was that grinning ape really dumb enough to think she liked him?

Everyone was gone now, everyone except for Kaine and the woman. He watched them come out of the house, the dog at Kaine's side. He was far enough out that the dog shouldn't notice the truck, but he squirmed, ready to pull out in an instant if he had to.

Kaine walked the woman to the car. *As if he'd be any protection to her.*

The man sneered and rubbed his hands together to warm them. Even with gloves, they were stiff from the cold. It wouldn't be long now, though. The woman was leaving.

He cracked the window on his side just enough to listen. The light, steady wind carried their voices. . . .

"What would it take to get you to sing again?"

Jennifer stared up at him. "Dan, I told you —"

"I know what you told me, Jennifer," he interrupted agreeably. "I'm just asking if there's any chance I could change your mind."

"None," she said without hesitating. "Why?"

Dan shrugged. "I'm going to combine the adult worship choir at church with my teen group at Easter for a musical. Having a trained voice to sing the part of Mary Magdalene would be a real plus."

"You've never heard me sing," Jennifer reminded him.

"You hum around the station all the time, didn't you know that? I recognize quality when I hear it."

"I — no. I'm sorry, Dan, but I can't."

He nodded as if he understood. "I don't suppose you'd want to listen to it before you give me a definite no, would you?"

"Dan, please —"

He tilted his head toward her as though he might continue to press. But then he smiled and touched her lightly on the arm. "OK. Listen, you be careful on the hill. It's a lot worse going down than coming up when it's this icy."

The man in the truck grimaced when he saw the woman place her hand over Kaine's just before she opened the car door. "I'll be fine," he heard her assure him. "Dan — thank you for tonight. No one's ever done anything like this for me before."

Kaine dropped the retriever's harness, ordered the dog to stay, then placed his hands on her shoulders.

She shouldn't let him touch her like that . . . she probably feels sorry for him . . . or aims to keep her job by playin' up to him. . . .

The man licked his lips, wishing he could hear what they were saying. But they were talking softer now, and the wind had shifted.

76

Is he going to kiss her?

No, she was getting in the car, starting the engine. Finally she pulled away and began to ease the car down the hill, leaving Kaine alone with the dog.

Suddenly the dog raised its head and turned toward the truck, lifting its ears as a menacing growl started in its throat. Kaine jerked his head around, too, and for an instant the man in the truck froze.

Then he remembered. Kaine couldn't see him. Kaine couldn't see anything.

He grinned as he suddenly brought the truck's engine to life with a thunderous roar. He cackled to himself and came charging out from the grove of pine trees, heading straight for the blind man and his dog.

He saw Kaine's mouth drop open, saw panic wash over his face, and he laughed even harder. He floored the accelerator and crushed the heel of his hand against the horn, skidding away from the blind man at the last possible minute, only seconds before he would have leveled him. The dog went crazy, snarling and barking like a wild thing.

That'll give him something to think about until I decide what I want to do next. . . .

FIVE

Ever since her welcome party three weeks before, Jennifer had been living in overdrive. She didn't mind; in fact, she thrived on it. The only thing that worried her was the amount of time she seemed to be spending with Dan — more specifically, how much she *enjoyed* the time she spent with Dan.

In addition to all the hours she was putting in on the radiothon, she now had the afternoon drive time each weekday. She jocked her own show, consisting mostly of contemporary and gospel music, public service announcements, and top-of-the-hour news. It was informal, fast-paced, and fun.

She was learning a lot, but she still had a lot more to learn. Because most of the station's procedures had been adapted to Dan's blindness, she had to take a slightly different approach to things she had once considered routine. With other tasks, she had to start from scratch.

She had recently mastered his Braillewriter and could now type messages directly into Braille. Gabe had taught her how to make up the special, raised version of the "hot clock" he had designed for Dan — a clever variation of the pie-chart broadcasting sched-

78

ule used by sighted disc jockeys. By now she had met most of the station's major advertisers, covered an assortment of community events, learned her way around town, and done a fifteen-minute feature on Helping Hand Farm after her visit with Dan and Jason.

One of the things she enjoyed most was something for which she received no salary. Along with several other volunteers from the station and the community, she donated a few hours each week as a reader for the closed-circuit radio service the station operated. The service provided over twenty hours of weekly broadcasting for the blind, furnishing receivers free of charge to those who couldn't afford to rent them.

In her spare time, she unpacked a box here and there. She was proud of the fact that after living in her little bungalow only six weeks, she had no more than four or five boxes left to empty.

She was also making lists. Jennifer had decided that she needed a strategy for organizing her life. She had bought a book on time management at the bookstore in the mall and was following it chapter by chapter, line by line. She was going to take this seriously, she promised herself. If she was going to be an efficient assistant, she needed to get organized.

At the moment, however, she was down on her hands and knees, burrowing in the bottom of her credenza. She was almost absolutely *positive* she had put the entire stack of Braille scheduling charts for the radiothon in there. But she had been so busy over the last few days, she had taken to tossing everything that didn't require immediate attention onto the same shelf. Now the charts were missing — if they had ever been there in the first place.

She grumbled to herself, then scrambled to her feet and turned around to — "Dan! Don't *do* that!"

He stood by her desk, looking mildly offended. "What exactly did I do?"

"You — *appeared.* You're so incredibly quiet. Clear your throat or something when my back is turned —" She grimaced. "Oh dear. I keep *doing* it! Of course, you don't know when my back is turned."

"Is your face red, Jennifer?"

"It certainly is. And so are my knees. I've been trying to find those schedules for the radiothon — the ones I typed on the Braillewriter for you."

"They're on my desk."

"Why are they on *your* desk?"

"Didn't you say you typed them for me?"

"Yes, but I put them in my office —"

"No you didn't. You put them on my desk." He shook his head sadly. "The mind is the first thing to go, kid."

"Not in my case. It's in better shape than my back."

"I have to go to the grocery store today." He said it with all the enthusiasm of a man facing an IRS audit.

Jennifer perched on the edge of her desk and grinned at him. She found Dan's strong dislike for grocery shopping both interesting and amusing. He had been known to resort to trickery, even bribery, to wheedle someone else into doing it for him. He had successfully used his routine on Jennifer two or three times. *But not today, Daniel,* she thought impishly. *Not today.*

"Fine," she said evenly. "I'll be happy to go along and help, if you like."

He had been expecting just that response, obviously, and jumped on it. "You sure you have the time?" Dan was a master of the thoughtful, concerned frown.

"Mm. No problem."

"I'm really pushed this afternoon. If you're sure you have time, I'll just give you my list. It's only half a dozen items or so." If a man's smile could be relieved, smug, and victorious all at the same time, Dan's was.

"No."

He looked surprised. "No, *what?*"

"No, I'm not doing your shopping. I did it last week — twice. I said I'd *help.* Today, we go together."

He pulled his mouth to one side as if considering his choices. "Why together? It would be more efficient for only one of us to go, wouldn't it? It would certainly save some time." He arched one heavy brow in his best "I'm trying to be reasonable" expression.

"For you, maybe. Not for me. It'll be faster for me if you go along," Jennifer said brightly. "You say you need half a dozen items. Fine — I'll pick up three, you get the other three. We'll be back at the station in twenty minutes flat."

He slumped but accepted defeat graciously. "You want to go now?"

"After lunch."

"I suppose I'm buying."

"Why, what a nice idea, Dan! I'll be ready in five minutes."

After a quick lunch at Papa Joe's, they headed for the shopping center. A few minutes later Jennifer pulled off the road into the parking lot, splashing through an enormous puddle. She squinted her eyes, peering through the rain-swept windshield.

"What is this, monsoon season?" she

grumbled. "Isn't there ever a happy medium in West Virginia's weather? Something a little less severe than blizzards and cloudbursts?"

Dan shrugged. "We'll have snow again by the end of the week. Maybe sooner."

She glanced over at him. "And that's our radar weather exclusive for today, folks. News at eleven."

"I'm as accurate as that guy on cable, the one who rhymes all his forecasts."

"True. But he's a great-looking guy."

"I would hope, Jennifer, that you're beyond being impressed by a handsome face."

"No woman can resist a true poet, Daniel."

"You actually watch that man?"

"Every evening at six. Faithfully."

He shook his head. "That's disgusting."

She grinned. "I'm going to let you and Sunny out at the door while I park. Otherwise, you'll both drown."

She waited until Sunny had guided Dan through the entrance of the supermarket before pulling away to look for a parking place. Finding nothing nearby, she nervously began to scout some of the rows farther out. It probably wasn't a good idea to leave Dan alone in the market too long, even with Sunny. He truly *did* get a little strange about shopping. She suspected he felt slightly less confident in stores than he liked to admit. Still, he had Sunny, so he'd be fine. . . .

A few minutes later, Jennifer rushed into the supermarket wringing water out of her drenched hair. She stood near the checkout lanes and scanned the front of the store for a glimpse of Dan and Sunny, finally locating them at a nearby produce bin. She started toward them but stopped a few feet away, intrigued by the curious scene taking place.

Dan, a somewhat grim smile on his face, was attempting to separate one flimsy plastic sack from another. With a soft grunt of frustration, he finally dropped Sunny's harness, pulled open the sack, and began to sort through the oranges in the case, squeezing them lightly before dropping one into the plastic bag.

Jennifer was about to move and offer her help when a short block of a woman with square shoulders and white hair done up in sausage-link curls walked up to Dan. She squinted up at him belligerently.

From her military stance at his right side, her head came only two or three inches above his waist. With a stern thrust of her chin, she gave a tug to her serviceable black raincoat and bellowed up at him in a voice that would have done a drill sergeant proud.

"You shouldn't squeeze them oranges!"

Dan, his hand suddenly suspended in mid-air over an orange, cocked his head to one side quizzically, then bent down toward her voice. "Ma'am?"

His small, polite smile faded when she repeated her warning, with some elaboration. "You'll bruise 'em! You pick good oranges by their color, not by the way they squeeze. Here, let me show you."

With no further fuss, she tucked her red umbrella under one arm and planted herself firmly next to Dan as she began to sort efficiently through the oranges. "Hmph! Men! Reckon your wife's at work."

Too surprised to resort to his usual sense of humor, Dan simply stood alongside her, his mouth slightly agape. "Uh . . . ma'am —"

"Sent you to do the shopping, did she? Well, you'd best go along with her a few times and learn how to do it proper! I wouldn't have turned my man — God rest his soul — loose at the market alone, not for anything. Look here, now!" She thrust a slightly mottled-looking orange directly upward to within an inch of Dan's nose. "See all those green places that're pushed in? You don't want that, no sir!"

Giving him no opportunity to react, she removed the bruised orange, trading it for a healthy one. "Here's a good one now. Well, open your *bag!*" Shaking her head with impatience, she plopped the large, perfect orange into the plastic sack still dangling from Dan's fingers. His mouth dropped open a little wider, but he said nothing.

Jennifer chewed the knuckles of her fist in a noble attempt to choke off a giggle, willfully choosing to ignore the small voice that prompted her to interrupt.

"Well, are you gonna finish gettin' what you want out of that bin, young man? I have some shopping of my *own* to tend to!" She hurled a withering look of disapproval at Dan.

"Oh — sure . . . yes, ma'am!" In his haste to oblige, Dan knocked one of the oranges from its fixed place on top of the rows. Twenty other round, ripe oranges promptly tumbled down and over the produce bin onto the floor.

Jennifer swallowed a groan of dismay and took a step forward, stopping again when Dan's accuser dropped quickly to her knees, hiking up her coat and dress enough to allow freedom of movement. Dan stood numbly mute, looking positively stricken.

"I swan, I don't know how some folks find their way home," the woman muttered, clucking her tongue in exasperation. With deft movements, she rolled a few oranges up onto her arm, then proceeded to bob up and down like a tightly compressed jack-in-the-box until she had replaced all the fruit in the bin. Waiting, Dan scratched his head, looked embarrassed, and reached for Sunny's harness.

Jennifer knew it was time to make an entrance. She fixed her face into what she hoped was a sober expression and approached the two of them. "Can I help?"

A quick look at Dan's scowling face confirmed what she feared — he had heard the snap of amusement in her voice. In a tone thick with menace, he leaned over and growled at her. "Where did you park — Cincinnati?"

"This your woman?" The fruit expert eyeballed Jennifer with disdain. "I'd handle the marketing myself, if I were you."

Jennifer swallowed almost painfully, halting the explosion of laughter that she knew would ruin her. "Ah . . . yes. Yes, I suppose I should," she said agreeably, meeting the woman's frown with a smile.

After this exchange, Dan squared his shoulders with dignity, cuddled the plastic sack of oranges to his chest, and pretended to glance innocently around at his surroundings.

"He's slow, is he?" The woman lowered her voice to a grating whisper.

"Slow?" Jennifer looked up into Dan's face, which was a classic study in self-control. "Well . . ."

The woman appraised Dan once more, without emotion, expelling a small grunt of sympathy for Jennifer. "I expect he's a handful, big boy like that." And with that sage pronouncement, she walked away.

It was Jennifer who finally broke the silence, dredging up every shred of self-control available to her in an effort to sound reasonably serious. "Well, Daniel, what else would you like besides oranges?"

"How long have you been standing there, Jennifer?" he asked in a deceptively mild voice, holding out the plastic sack to her as though it might be contaminated.

Jennifer meekly took the bag. "How long? Oh — well, you see, Dan, I had to look for a parking place. I was hurrying — I know how much you hate being alone in the supermarket — when I saw this elderly lady trying to juggle her cane and umbrella in the parking lot. She had dropped her sack, and her groceries were spilling out into a puddle. I had to help her, of course. I couldn't just leave her there like that. I thought you'd be all right, since Sunny was with you."

"That's good, kid. Very good," he said in a nasty tone of voice. "Go on. I can't *wait* to hear the rest of this."

"Daniel, it's *true,* honestly, I'm telling you —"

"How long, Jennifer?"

She took a deep breath, prepared for his wrath — which, she had to admit, was deserved. "I don't think I missed too much, actually." She bit her bottom lip and waited expectantly. "Are you angry with me?"

"Angry?" he repeated smoothly, flinging an arm around her shoulder and giving her a rather rough hug. "Oh, I don't get angry, Jennifer —"

"I just get even," she echoed in unison with him.

"You're doing better, though," he said.

"What?"

"Well, I was expecting you to tear into that poor little old lady with your standard lecture on how to treat the disabled." He gave her a tolerant smile. "I think it's actually a healthy sign that you were able to stand there and enjoy my misery, Jennifer."

He laughed at her small, disgruntled sound of self-defense. "C'mon, kid. I'll show you how to handpick the finest apples in the county."

Before they left the shopping center, Jennifer coaxed Dan into a quick visit to the pet shop. He did everything he could to talk her into taking home a cross-eyed Siamese kitten that stole her heart as soon as she walked up to its cage, but she reluctantly left it there.

"I don't know if I can have pets or not. It didn't even occur to me to ask when I rented the house." She glanced behind her as they went out the door.

"Well, why don't you find out? Joe Como is so taken with you, he'd let you stock your own ark if it made you happy."

Once inside the car, Jennifer stared out at the dismal afternoon and the cold rain still falling steadily. "Another few hours of this, and the ark might be a real possibility."

It was only a little after three, but the slate gray sky and the downpour made it look more like evening. Jennifer drove with the headlights on dim and the windshield wipers on high.

Dan contentedly helped himself to a half-pound bag of chocolate-covered peanuts. "Want some?"

Jennifer glanced at the candy with longing. "They make me hyper," she said ruefully, scooping out a handful.

"What doesn't?"

Ignoring him, she turned off the main

highway onto the two-lane county road that provided a shortcut to the radio station. "I don't know . . . maybe I should have stayed on the Drive. Visibility is zilch, and I hate this road."

"It's getting colder, too," Dan said. "Better watch the bridge — it might be slick."

Jennifer glanced in the rearview mirror. There wasn't another car in sight. "Looks like everyone else had sense enough to stay home today."

They lapsed into silence for the next few minutes, listening to the station and munching peanuts. The new disc jockey was doing part of Jennifer's show in her absence.

"He's not nearly as good as you are, you know," Dan finally said, breaking the quiet.

"Why, Daniel — and I thought you hadn't noticed." Jennifer attempted to cover the warm rush of pleasure she felt at his compliment.

"Mm. I notice more than you think. Our advertising has increased quite a bit for that afternoon drivetime. Started about a week after you took the show."

"Aha! *That's* why you noticed. Money talks."

He shrugged. "You're good. You've got a lot of class on the air. You're easy on the ears, witty —" He paused. "Your voice . . .

grabs people. Holds them. I think they hear the same thing in it I do."

"What?"

"The smile in your voice," Dan replied simply. "Were you smiling just now?"

"Yes," answered Jennifer slowly. "How did you know?"

"I can hear it. I don't have to see your smile to feel it. And I think our listeners feel it, too."

Flustered, Jennifer tried to pass the moment off lightly. She looked at him out of the corner of her eye. "Your shopping is done, so that's not your game. What are you up to, boss?"

Dan closed the candy sack and stashed it between them on the console. "There *is* something I'd like to talk about."

Instantly alert to the gravity of his tone, Jennifer nodded. "I knew it."

She glanced sideways to see him lace his fingers together and crack his knuckles, an uncommon gesture for Daniel. "Jennifer . . . how would you feel about . . . going out with me?"

"Going out with you?" Jennifer parroted his words, trying to concentrate on the highway, which was beginning to reflect a suspicious-looking glaze. It was sleeting. She moaned aloud.

"Sorry — it was just an idea." Dan's face went immediately slack.

"What — oh, no! I didn't mean —"

"It's OK," he said quickly. "I don't always read signals right. My mistake."

"Dan —" Jennifer reached out to touch his arm — "I was groaning because it's *sleeting* and the road is horrendous. Not because you asked me out!"

He said nothing. Jennifer looked over at him again, bewildered by the unmistakable tension lining his face. He looked as if he were about to jump from the car.

Daniel Kaine? *Insecure?*

Understanding finally dawned. "You're asking me for a date, is that it?"

"In my own inimitable way," Daniel said dryly after a noticeable hesitation.

"Oh." Jennifer bit her lower lip.

Well, why not? A date was only a date, after all. She spent most of her waking hours with him as it was. What would be so different about a date?

An alarm sounded somewhere in Jennifer's head. She was already too attracted to Dan and spent far too much time with him. An honest-to-goodness date would only intensify an already treacherous situation, and she really shouldn't. It would definitely not be a smart thing to do.

"Of course I'll go out with you, Dan," she said softly. "I'd like that very much."

He cracked his knuckles again. "Look, you don't have to say yes just because you work for me. I wouldn't —"

"I didn't."

"Didn't what?"

"Say yes just because I work for you."

"Well, there *are* drawbacks, Jennifer. I'm not exactly your conventional date."

"I don't know that that's necessarily a drawback, Dan."

"You'd have to pick me up, you know."

"That's hardly a problem."

"And Sunny goes with me."

"Sunny and I are pals. What evening did you have in mind?"

"We could ask Gabe and Lyss to come along. That way you wouldn't have to drive —"

"I enjoy driving. When?"

"Look, Jennifer, I want to be sure you understand that —"

"*When,* Daniel?"

He grinned, relaxed his hands, and drew a long breath. "My mother does that."

"Your mother does what?" Jennifer asked impatiently.

"Calls me *Daniel* in that tone of voice when she gets impatient with me. How about tomorrow night?"

"It's a weeknight."

He was instantly wary. "You're busy?"

"Not unless you make me work overtime again, I'm not. Fine. Tomorrow night. But only if I can leave the station by five."

"Four, if you like."

"Deal. Just to satisfy my curiosity, why were you so uptight about asking me for a date?"

"I wasn't uptight. What makes you think I was uptight?"

"Your lips turned blue and you broke the knuckles on both hands."

"I always do that. It doesn't mean I'm uptight."

Jennifer waited.

His expression sobered. "I just wasn't sure if you would want to. The employer-employee thing." He turned his face toward the window on his side. "And the blindness," he added, his voice lower. "There's not exactly a waiting list of women wanting to go out with a blind man. I'm sure you can imagine some of the possible complications."

Jennifer remained silent for a moment. "Well, I think I can handle most of those . . . complications by now, don't you?" she asked evenly. "Since we're together so much?"

He turned toward her. "You're really comfortable with the idea?"

Jennifer considered her reply. There were times when she felt distinctly *uncomfortable* with Dan. Unsettled. Even disturbed. But she knew it had nothing to do with his blindness. It had more to do, she suspected uneasily, with some new and unfamiliar emotions that wouldn't seem to give her any peace these days.

She hoped she didn't sound evasive. "I'd say so. I —" She swallowed the rest of her words as she glanced out the side mirror. A pickup truck was moving up rapidly behind them. Too rapidly. She saw him skid on the slippery road once. Then again. But he continued to close in on them. Jennifer's hands tensed on the steering wheel.

"What's wrong?" Dan asked, immediately alert to the tension in her.

"I *hate* it when people do that! There's a pickup truck right on my bumper."

"Maybe if you slow down he'll go around."

Jennifer glanced down at the speedometer and eased up on the gas pedal. When she looked in the mirror again, the truck had slowed down, too. He was staying right with her.

She slowed even more. So did the truck.

"Is he still tailgating you?"

"Yes. And he's making me extremely nervous. There's ice on the road, and it's not safe —"

"Pull off, why don't you? Let him pass."

"I think I will. He's getting a little too close." She turned on her right blinker and slowed even more, easing the car over to the shoulder of the road.

By the time Dan heard the sound of the truck's engine, it was too late. It was the same truck, he was certain of it. There was the choppy, distinctive miss of a blown head gasket and the additional loud whirring of something loose or broken under the hood. The sound he had heard the night of Jennifer's party. The sound of the truck that had tried to run him down — or at least had tried to make him *think* it was going to run him down.

"Jennifer, watch out —"

The warning came a second too late. He felt the jolt, the sudden push from the rear on Jennifer's side of the car, heard the loud crunch of metal. The car went pitching off the pavement and into a ditch. He snaked out one hand to help her steady the wheel and cried out a sharp warning. "Don't brake! Go with it!"

He heard her ragged breathing, heard her gasp for air, but he could tell by the way she was gripping the wheel that she hadn't panicked. The sudden, careening stop knocked his arm sharply against hers, but they were all right.

He heard the truck go on by, heard the sound of the motor gradually fade as it roared on down the road. His hands were shaking as he released his seat belt and reached for her.

"Jennifer —"

"Oh, Dan — are you all right?"

"I'm fine. What about you?" he asked gruffly, gripping her hand.

For a second, they both sat speechless and stunned. Then Jennifer unlocked her seat belt and fought for a couple of deep breaths. Without a second thought, Dan ignored the console and reached across the seat, gathering her into his arms.

Jennifer's tenuous self-control shattered, and she choked on a ragged sob. Dan felt his own hands tremble as he tried to calm her. He held her for a long time, pressing her face against his shoulder, murmuring soft sounds of comfort against her hair.

"It's OK, now. We're fine, honey, we're just fine."

"But it must be awful for you." Her voice

sounded strangled against his shoulder. "Another car accident after what happened before. . . ."

Dan shushed her gently, smiling to think that, after what had just happened, her primary concern was for him. He cradled her tightly against his chest, rocking her back and forth as he would a child.

"I'm perfectly fine," he assured her. "Gabe has given me a couple of much bigger scares in his old T-bird. Don't even think about it."

"But, Dan, that was *deliberate!* That truck intentionally rammed into us!"

"Are you sure, Jennifer?" But he knew the answer to his own question. *He might have really hurt someone this time,* he thought. A cold trickle of fear iced the back of his neck as he realized that *someone* could have been Jennifer. What was he going to do about this nut? He couldn't just let it go on.

"Did you get a good look at the truck?" he asked her. "License number, anything?"

"No," she said. "It was an old pickup, that's all I noticed. A Ford, I think."

He had known it was a truck, had known by the sound of it that night when the guy came barreling over the hill at him. But another Ford? He swallowed hard. *Just a weird coincidence, that's all. There must be hun-*

dreds of Ford pickups in this county.

He cupped the back of her head again. "Shh . . . there's nothing we can do about it now. He's long gone. We'd better get back on the road. Are you OK to drive?"

Drawing away from him, Jennifer sniffed a few times. He heard her fishing for a tissue. She blew her nose, then expelled a long breath. "Yes, I'm all right. We're in a ditch, but I think I can get out. It's not that deep."

She moved away from him, and he heard the click of her seat belt. After several minutes of rocking the car from reverse to drive, they were out of the ditch and back on the road.

In the silence on the way back to the station, Dan could hear Jennifer's anxious breathing. Twice he heard her seat creak as she turned to look back over her shoulder. And he understood. If he hadn't been blind, he would have been looking over *his* shoulder, too.

SIX

During the next few days Jennifer found herself growing increasingly concerned about Dan's peculiar quietness. He was pensive, unusually serious — even moody, she thought. Two or three times she had walked into his office and found him sitting at his desk, raking his hands through his beard in a gesture of weariness and frowning as if he were worried about something. When she tried to get him to talk about it, he pretended he didn't know what she meant and quickly changed the subject.

The only times Jennifer had been with him over the past week had been during work hours at the station or on a work-related project. Objectively, she knew that shouldn't concern her. Still, she couldn't help but wonder why he had suddenly become so distant.

Today had been no different. They had been on the church bus for over half an hour on their way to a youth rally in Clarksburg, and he had spoken no more than two or three sentences the entire time. She had helped him enough with the ensemble to know he was usually buoyant and full of fun when he was with the teens. At the moment, however, he seemed distracted and almost lethargic.

"Does Gabe always drive the bus?" she asked, making yet another attempt at conversation.

For a moment, she thought he hadn't heard her. But he finally answered. "Most of the time," he said.

Something about his hands caught Jennifer's attention. They were clenched tightly in his lap, and every now and then he would squeeze them together as though they ached.

Her gaze moved back to his face. "Jason is having a great time up there with Jim Arbegunst and the other fellows. Do you usually bring him with you to these rallies?"

Dan nodded. "When we can. He likes being with the teens. They give him a lot of attention."

"The ensemble is providing all the music tonight?"

"Mm-hm."

Another long interval of silence followed. Jennifer glanced across the aisle to the other window, staring out with no real interest at the rugged, mountainous landscape. It had turned cold again, and the contoured hillsides were snow-covered against a deep gray winter's sky.

"I think it's going to snow again."

Dan made no reply. Finally Jennifer decided she'd had enough. "Dan, are you upset about something?" she demanded bluntly.

That seemed to get his attention. He relaxed his hands as if he had only then noticed what he was doing and turned his face toward her. He looked surprised.

"Upset?"

"You're awfully quiet. In fact, you've been quiet all week. Is something wrong?"

He frowned and shook his head. "No. I'm sorry, I guess I've just had a lot on my mind."

"Are you angry with me?"

His look of surprise returned. "Why would I be angry with you?"

"I don't know." Jennifer thought for a moment. "I did nag you about calling the police last week, after that truck ran us off the road. I still don't understand why you wouldn't report it."

"I told you why," he said tightly. "It wouldn't have done any good."

Dan immediately regretted his shortness with her. He softened his voice. "We didn't even have a license number, remember? There are a lot of Ford pickup trucks in this county."

"Well, I still think we should have told the police."

Dan could hear the slight edge in her voice and knew she didn't understand. Why should she? More to the point, how *could* she?

He wasn't even sure *he* understood. None of it made any sense. He was beginning to feel like a marked man. Ever since the incident with the truck last week, the phone calls had been coming more frequently, almost regularly. And each time he had had the peculiar sensation that the caller was angrier and more disturbed than ever. Worse still, he'd had the distinct feeling at least twice this week that someone was watching the house. He had tried to tell himself he was just going through another round of anxiety attacks. But he wondered.

The man called the house every night, sometimes more than once. Occasionally, he spoke; more often he didn't. He had begun calling the station almost daily. But he never came right out and explained what he was up to. Over and over, Dan had asked himself whether the caller actually meant him harm, or whether he was simply trying to frighten him. Or, even more likely, if he was just a loose cannon looking for a target.

He also wondered if there was any significance to the fact that as the radiothon drew nearer, the harassment seemed to intensify. A connection seemed unlikely, yet he was beginning to suspect that there might be one. Could the idea of the radiothon possibly be so abhorrent to someone that he would go to this length to stop it?

He found that hard to believe. Yet he couldn't shake the feeling that in some way the radiothon was at the heart of this siege of madness.

If he were right, he knew he would have to tell someone soon, no matter how odious he found the idea. Too many people were involved in the radiothon. He couldn't let his own stubborn independence overshadow common sense. If he waited too long and this turned out to be more than a scare tactic, he might put someone else in jeopardy.

Someone like Jennifer.

The thought stabbed him in the heart.

He reached over and covered her hand with his. "I'm sorry. I guess I *have* been preoccupied," he said softly, turning toward her. "You have to understand. There's this lady in my life who's messing up my head. I seem to have a lot of trouble thinking of anything else but her these days."

"You needn't apologize," she murmured. "I know you're busy."

He squeezed her hand. "Am I forgiven?"

She pressed her fingers against his but said nothing.

Jennifer and Dan started through the entrance of the host church while Jim took Sunny for a pit stop. Distracted for an instant when Gabe yelled a question at them from the bus, Jennifer turned back to Dan, only to see him narrowly miss being hit in the face by the swinging church door.

She started to cry out a warning, but it died on her lips as he pivoted smoothly away from the door, narrowly avoiding its impact.

"How did you do that?"

"Do what?" Dan waited for her to guide him down the hall to the auditorium. "I wish Jim would bring Sunny on back. I could use her for a while."

"You've done it before," Jennifer said, bending over to pick up some music she'd dropped. She tucked her free hand under his arm and began to walk with him. "You avoid collisions as if you could see them coming."

"I have facial vision," he replied.

Just then, Jim and the retriever came through the door, and Jennifer waited while Dan put Sunny's harness on.

"What's facial vision?"

"Radar," Dan said shortly, allowing Sunny to lead him up the steps to the platform.

Jennifer stared at him for a moment, then

followed. "Figures," she muttered dryly. "Batman and Robin together again."

"Great team," he answered cheerfully. "Jim, if you're going back to the bus, tell Gabe I need him in here as soon as possible to help set up the sound.

"It really is a kind of radar," he went on to explain to Jennifer. "Bats have it. When objects — or people — move, they send out sound waves. If you really work at it, you get to the point where you can estimate the size of an object. It's helped to save my head a number of times."

He stood unmoving for a moment, as if trying to get his bearings. "Give me the layout of the platform, would you? I haven't been here for over a year. I don't especially want to provide any unexpected entertainment for all these teenagers by falling on my face."

"You're at the front right now." Jennifer glanced around them. "There's nothing up here except a grand piano and a console organ a few feet to your left. And there's a podium at the far left front. Of course, we haven't got any of our stuff in place yet." She opened his music case and searched until she found the program for the evening, which she had typed into Braille for him.

Jason came bounding up the steps just

then, screeching to a sudden halt in front of Dan. He started to pet Sunny, then stopped.

"Dan, can I take Sunny off her harness and keep her with me?"

"No. Remember what I told you about that, Jason," Dan said firmly, squatting down on one knee by the retriever. "Sunny has a job to do, and she expects to take her orders from me. When the harness is on, that means she's working and can't play. When I take it off, she knows it's all right to have fun."

"Oh yeah . . . I forgot. You're her boss."

"Something like that." Dan stood, hooking his thumb in the harness.

"And you're Jennifer's boss, too." A frown ridged Jason's forehead. "How does *she* know when it's all right to play?"

Dan lifted one dark eyebrow in obvious amusement. "Ah . . . right. Well, you see, Jason, Jennifer likes her work so much she's always having fun." He turned around with a smug grin. "Isn't that right, Jennifer?"

Jennifer crossed her arms over her ski jacket and weighed her answer carefully. "That's exactly right, Jason," she declared, watching Dan incline his head in anticipation. "That's why I work so much overtime. It's strictly for *fun.*"

"*Dan —*" Jason shifted impatiently from

one foot to the other.

"All right, all right. Take her and go." Dan removed Sunny's harness and hustled the dog and the boy off with a grin. "But stay close to Jim."

The boy hesitated. "Will you be OK, Dan? Without Sunny?"

"I'll be just fine, sport," Dan said with a smile. "Jennifer will be my eyes for now."

As Jason and the retriever took off, Dan turned slightly, raising his chin in the alert, listening expression he often wore. "So — what do you think of my little buddy?"

"Oh, he's adorable! It's just too bad. . . ."

Dan's smile faded. "Too bad?"

"You know — that he's the way he is." Jennifer had heard the tone of his voice change and glanced up at him.

"Retarded, you mean?"

Jennifer wondered at the somber expression on his face. "Dan? Did I say something wrong?"

"No. Not really." His smile was strained and quickly gone. "I'll be honest with you. That phrase — *it's too bad* — has been a pet peeve of mine ever since the accident. I understand it bothers a lot of people with disabilities. It's . . . a little like someone raking long fingernails across a blackboard, you know?"

She saw him clench and unclench his right hand as he went on. "A quadriplegic I met through Friend-to-Friend told me it always made him think of a gaggle of mourners standing over a coffin and clucking their tongues over the body."

Embarrassed, Jennifer bit her lower lip nervously. "I'm so sorry. I didn't know."

His mouth softened to a more natural smile. "You couldn't. Don't worry about it. Sometimes I overreact. But what you said about Jason . . ." He hesitated, took a deep breath, then exhaled slowly.

"Dan, I didn't mean to —"

He dismissed her protest with a wave of his hand. "I understand what you meant. But I don't agree with you. I guess I don't think about Jason as being — deprived. Just special."

"Are you saying it doesn't bother you that Jason is so . . . *limited?*" she asked incredulously.

He shrugged. "You tell me, Jennifer — is Jason really so much worse off than other kids? Than *normal* kids?"

"But he's such a beautiful little boy!" Jennifer countered sharply. "Doesn't it make you angry, Daniel, seeing the unfairness of his life? Doesn't it hurt you, knowing he's — trapped like that?"

"Trapped?" Something flickered in his eyes — the eyes that usually held only tenderness or laughter or concern — and his chin lifted just a fraction.

"Well," she stammered uncertainly, "he's never going to be able to lead a normal life."

Dan's jaw tensed even more. "You see Jason as a tragedy, do you?"

"I — no! That's not what I meant, I —"

"No? What, then?"

She heard the accusation in his voice, saw a muscle tighten at the corner of his mouth. The conversation had suddenly gone wrong, and she hurried to end it.

"I think it's so unfair, that's all," she murmured. "I don't understand why God allows some of the things he allows —"

Dan moved just a step closer to her and straightened his shoulders. Then, unexpectedly, his expression began to gentle and his mouth curved into a thoughtful smile. "And you'd like to correct a few of his mistakes, wouldn't you?" he asked quietly.

"What?"

"Let's forget it," he suggested abruptly, still smiling.

"Not until you explain that last remark." Jennifer dug in, not about to budge.

He remained silent for a moment. Then a familiar glint of amusement crossed his face. "You're such a rebel," he said mildly, reaching out to entwine a strand of her hair around his finger. "In the sixties, you would have spent most of your time at sit-ins and protest marches, I'll bet." With a small nod of his head, he added, "Instead, you're stuck with an exasperating blind man and a mentally limited little boy. No real challenge for a gal with a burning heart."

"At least you didn't say *bleeding* heart," she muttered grudgingly.

"Now you're angry with me." Suddenly he looked extremely vulnerable.

"No." Jennifer found it next to impossible to be genuinely angry with Dan, even though he *could* be the most exasperating man at times. But for now, she could feel her petulance fading as she studied him.

His face was so . . . *endearing,* she thought. It was the face of a man who had known great pain and enormous loss, yet had miraculously retained the ability to laugh deeply and live — even love — fully. Shadows had marched across that face, but they had been powerless to destroy the light of the man. A quiet flame glowed from within, the subtle blending of gentleness and strength, humor and kindness, that made him Daniel Kaine.

"Jennifer, I wasn't criticizing you." He spread his hands with apology. "We just look

112

at things differently. You see Jason as trapped. I don't. If I did, I'd have to see myself the same way . . . and I don't dare.

"That boy," he continued quietly, "has a precious gift of wonder. He appreciates all the little ordinary things that other people never even notice. To Jason, a colored rock is a special gift. A seashell is magic. A butterfly is a friend. And life is . . . pure, unqualified joy."

The warmth in his tone deepened, and tenderness filled his smile. "He has a faith that you and I can only envy. He *knows* the Father. He holds God's hand, talks to him about every little thing in his life — frogs and rainbows and ladybugs, the dream he had last night, the scrape on his knee, the hurt in his heart." Dan shook his head in a knowing gesture of affection.

"I believe that Jason says 'I love you' to the Lord with every breath he takes. He has an enormous capacity — and a tremendous need — for love. Just like all of us," he added quietly.

Jennifer lowered her eyes to stare at the floor. She suddenly felt terribly young and insensitive.

"Do you really think," he asked, his voice deep with emotion, "that's what it's like to be trapped?"

"I'm sorry, Dan," Jennifer choked out. "Obviously, I don't know what I'm talking about."

"You *are* upset with me. Don't be," he urged her. "I hate it when your voice loses its smile."

She looked away from him, feeling a sudden need to hide her agitation, even though she knew he couldn't see her face. "No. Really, I'm not!" she protested, trying to force a note of brightness into her words.

He stood unmoving, as though he were attempting to search her mind, to probe the corners of her heart. Neither of them spoke for a long time.

Suddenly she felt his hands on her shoulders, a light, uncertain touch. Then he tipped her chin upward, forcing her to face him. Jennifer caught her breath. The tenderness in his expression made her heart ache.

"Jennifer," he said very quietly, his hands tightening on her shoulders, "I wish I could find a way to convince you to let go of your anger."

"Anger?" Again she looked away, unable to endure the depth of feeling that had settled over his features.

He nodded sadly. "Anger. That's what it is, you know. You're angry with God. About your singing career. My blindness. Jason. So many things.

"You think God is unfair. So you beat your fists against his will." His expression was gentle, his tone firm but not censuring. "It doesn't work, Jennifer. I can tell you from experience that being angry with God doesn't work." He brushed her cheek lightly with one finger. "He's not your enemy, Jennifer."

Jennifer tensed under his hands. She didn't want to argue with him. She didn't want to explain herself or try to defend herself. Dan was right about the anger, but she didn't want him to know the extent of it. She didn't want to expose the barrenness of her spirit to a man whose faith seemed to scale mountains and soar with the eagles.

Ridiculously, she almost wished him less than he was, a weaker man, because suddenly she wanted desperately to be big enough for him, to be *good* enough for him.

She knew that any woman who would love this man would have to have wings on her faith, wings that would enable her to rise above the shadows and fly beyond the darkness.

Unfortunately, the wings of *her* faith were pitifully weak. Perhaps even irreparably broken.

SEVEN

When they stepped outside three hours later, they were met by an angry blast of wind and swirling snow. Obviously, the snow had been falling for some time; the ground was already covered.

"I simply love this weather," Jennifer muttered.

"Might as well get used to it," Dan said. He slung one arm around her shoulder as he held Sunny's harness with the other hand.

Jennifer wrinkled her nose and squinted her eyes against the pelting snow. Ahead of them, Gabe was hustling everyone onto the bus, growling out orders to speed up the loading of equipment. The teens, trying to meet his demands, were running back and forth from the bus to the auditorium, sliding and skating on the pavement as they tugged their instruments up the steps of the bus.

Jennifer brushed snow from her hair and face as she followed Dan and Sunny down the aisle. On the way, she exchanged wisecracks with the teens who were already on board. She stopped long enough to settle Jason into a seat beside Jim before going on to the rear of the bus to sit with Dan.

He waited until she scooted in next to the

window, then coiled his long frame into the seat beside her, with Sunny settling herself in the aisle by his side. "This may be a long ride," he said, opening the cover of his Braille watch and touching its face. "We'll be lucky to get home by one if the roads are as bad as Gabe thinks they're going to be."

The words were no more out of his mouth than Gabe stood up from the driver's seat and turned to face his passengers, giving the zipper of his coat a sharp tug. His voice was unusually serious and authoritative. "People, I want you to do your driver a big favor. Just lean back, relax — and sack out! Beginning now. This is *not* a good night for giving old Gabe a hard time. In fact, I strongly recommend that you don't even breathe too heavy."

The request was unnecessary. Most of the teens, already drowsy from the late hour and the rich food they had eaten after the rally, fell asleep within minutes.

Lulled by the warmth from the heater and the monotonous roar of the tires on the snow-covered road, Jennifer felt her eyes growing heavy. Even so, she made an attempt to carry on a conversation with Dan.

"You look tired, Daniel."

"I am." With a large, contented yawn, he leaned his head back against the seat, turning his face to Jennifer. "You?" He reached for her, wrapping her slender hand snugly inside the warmth of his larger one.

"Because my speech is slurred and my eyes won't focus? Of course not. Comatose, maybe, but not tired."

He laughed softly. "I'll lend you a shoulder if you want to take a nap."

"Mm . . . you're tempting me, Dan, you really are." Jennifer's voice thickened as she fought to keep her eyes open.

"My pleasure," he assured her in a whisper, his free hand gently coaxing her head onto the broad warmth of his shoulder.

"I probably can't sleep, you know," Jennifer protested with a huge yawn, trying hard to ignore the crazy flip-flop of her heart. She glanced uneasily over her shoulder at the icy window beside her. Snow was pelting the bus, driven by a moaning, angry wind.

Shivering, she nestled a little closer to Dan's warmth. "Bad weather always makes me nervous."

"Anything you can't fix makes you nervous, rebel. Go to sleep. The Lord can handle this one without your help."

Too tired to protest, Jennifer yawned again. "Mm-hmm . . . I s'pose. . . ."

Dan smiled with enormous pleasure, lean-

118

ing closer to accommodate Jennifer's head on his shoulder. He felt like a king as she leaned contentedly against him. He touched his cheek to her hair, and the soft fragrance made him almost dizzy.

It occurred to him that this was probably one of the few times Jennifer wasn't actively protesting . . . *something* . . . and he smiled.

She moved her hand, bringing it to lie against his chest as she stirred in her sleep. He covered it with his own, curling her slender fingers under his as though he were sheltering a small dove beneath his palm.

Please, Lord, let it be her . . . after all these years of waiting, being afraid to hope and being afraid not *to . . . please, let her be the one.*

Within moments, he closed his eyes and fell asleep.

Jennifer awoke to the engine drone that had soothed her to sleep. She looked up at Dan from under heavy-lidded eyes, her heartbeat quickening when she saw the tender way he had locked her hand in his. A warm blanket of sweetness enfolded her as she gazed up into his sleeping face. His silken charcoal hair was ruffled from sleep, falling away from his face instead of forward as it usually did.

In the rare vulnerability of the moment,

she thought she could detect just a glimpse of the boy he had once been. A tendril of sadness coiled around her heart as she studied him. What was it like for him when he woke up morning after morning to the same gray void — always the same, whether he was awake or asleep? How did he face day after day of getting up in the dark . . . going to bed with no moonlight creeping through his window, no stars to wish on? How did he live, knowing it would never again be daylight for him?

Such a good, kind man, Lord, she thought sadly, unaware for a moment that she was praying. *Why did this have to happen to him? With all the cruel, wicked people in this world — people who bring nothing but misery to others — why did such a terrible thing have to happen to Dan?*

A familiar well of bitterness bubbled up in her again, and her thoughts turned even more resentful. *Why Daniel . . . or Loren . . . or my mother . . . or little Jason? Not one of them ever did a mean thing in their lives.*

A random thought of her own personal hurt insinuated itself among the others — her dream, her special, bright, shining dream. The focus of her life had been to sing, to bring people to their feet in awe of the music, the glorious music. . . .

I won't think about it. I promised myself I'd never think about it.

She looked up at Dan again. Odd, how in such a short time she had come to count on this man, to trust him and believe in him when she couldn't seem to believe in much of anything else. She thought she could literally throw her life into his hands with complete confidence. What a strange, inexplicable way to feel about — a blind man.

Suddenly, an old, bittersweet memory drifted into her mind, a memory touched with pain and poignant with love. She saw her mother's face, frail and white and drawn in the last remaining days of her life. She heard the strained voice, once so melodious and resonant, now drained of its rich, vibrant strength. And she saw herself, a frightened, angry teenager, fighting to hold on to her mother. To the end, she had gone on fighting. . . .

It was one of the last times they had prayed together, and Jennifer had had to force herself to keep her head bowed and her thoughts turned to God. She was so terribly angry by then. And afraid. Afraid of what was coming, the suffering her small mother would yet endure, the desperate loneliness her father would have to bear, the adolescent

Paul's confusion, and poor little Loren's bewilderment. Loren had been unable to understand, at only eight years old, why his irritable, anxious older sister was suddenly doing all the things for him his mommy had once done.

In spite of her weakness, her mother's voice had been surprisingly strong that day.

". . . Jennifer is such a good girl, Father, a strong girl. She will need a strong man, Lord. I know that even now you are preparing such a man for her, just as you're preparing Jennifer for her future husband. I pray that he will be a very special man, Father . . . very special indeed, for Jennifer is special, too."

She had opened her eyes then and looked directly into Jennifer's gaze, her frail hand clasping her daughter's even tighter. "You must be sure to wait, Jennifer. Wait for God's man."

Unhappy, sick with pity and worry for her mother, Jennifer had only managed a disinterested mumble. "Yes, Mother. I will."

Her mother had smiled then, her eyes brimming with love and certainty. "He'll be . . . different, I imagine; no ordinary man. The Lord knows you need a strong, different kind of man to help you harness that independent spirit of yours and bring it into line for God's work." She had moved her hand to Jennifer's cheek, still smiling into her daughter's eyes. "You wait and see, Jennifer. He'll be a very special man. . . ."

Suddenly, Jennifer looked up at Dan and felt a need to touch him. She reached out to smooth a dark wisp of hair away from his forehead, and he slowly opened his eyes. He squeezed her hand, his slow, gentle smile enveloping her in its warmth.

"I didn't mean to wake you," Jennifer murmured. She thought she should probably move away, but she felt a sudden sense of loss at the very thought.

Had her mind not been so thick with fatigue and clouded with memories, she might have felt a trace of amazement at how easy it was, how right it felt, to be almost in his arms. Indeed, she *was* in his arms, she suddenly realized, with one hand against his chest, still tucked inside his, and his other arm now coming to rest securely around her shoulders. But she felt not even the slightest inclination to move away.

"Is it still snowing?" he asked softly.

"Are you admitting a radar failure?" she teased in a whisper. Glancing out of the corner of her eye — as much effort as she could bring herself to make at the moment — she shuddered at the lack of visibility.

"It's *awful!* I can't see anything."

He gently cupped her shoulder with his hand, moving her closer to him until her face was almost touching his. "Then don't look," he said softly, smiling the irresistible slow smile she had grown to cherish so very much.

Jennifer was unable to look away from his face. They were so close, their lips almost brushing. But still they didn't touch. She sensed that he was waiting, wondering, and she felt herself dropping deeper into the dark stillness wrapped around them.

"Is the gang still asleep?" he finally whispered, moving his hand from her shoulder to lift and comb gently through the tousled waves of her hair.

"I think so. Hard to believe so many teenagers can all conk out at once, isn't it?" Jennifer felt an irrational urge to start babbling, to chatter away the sweet intensity of the moment.

"No one's awake but us?" His voice was low, so low it made her catch her breath.

"Just . . . us," she answered weakly. "And Gabe, I hope." Her words stuck in her throat when he began, with an achingly gentle touch, to trace the pattern of her face. His rough fingertips traveled over her smooth skin, lingering on her lips. "Why?" she choked out.

"Because . . ." The word was no more than a whisper as his thumb tenderly rubbed across her dimpled chin. "I don't especially want an audience the first time I kiss you."

Jennifer saw his eyelashes flutter uncertainly against the upper ridge of his cheekbones. His hands framed her face as he lowered his head. At last he found her lips, touching them with his own in a kiss as light as a whisper.

Jennifer's heart seemed to melt like a low-burning candle when Dan breathed her name, just once, against the softness of her cheek. She could hear her pulse pound in her ears, the only sound around them in the darkness.

He gathered her as close as the seat would allow, kissing her once more, a longer kiss of tenderness and searching and meaning. When he finally put her gently away from him, Jennifer heard him sigh as though it made him very sad.

"Ah, Jennifer," he whispered against her cheek, "you are such a gift . . . such a precious gift."

"Daniel —" She reached up to touch the textured velvet of his bearded cheek, and he quickly covered her hand with his own.

"So fine," he murmured. "Everything about you is so . . . *fine* . . . *so beautiful* . . .

and you don't even know it. You have no idea how very precious you are . . . especially to me."

Jennifer's head suddenly began to pound. *It can't be Daniel, Lord . . . it can't be him, can it? He's strong — but he's too strong. Far too strong for me. I could never be what he needs, what he deserves. Never. I don't understand this man, I don't understand his strength or his obedience to you or his peace. It can't be Daniel . . . that wouldn't work at all, Lord . . . it just wouldn't work at all.*

She buried her head in the warmth of Dan's shoulder, ignoring — for the moment at least — how very different they were from each other and the thought of how impossible it would ever be to reconcile those differences.

EIGHT

The man leaned back as far as possible against the torn seat of the truck. The streetlight wasn't shining directly on him, but it was shedding enough of a glow to make him nervous.

He chewed his lower lip anxiously with his teeth, then sneered at his own skittishness. No one was paying any attention to the truck. Kaine couldn't see anything, and the woman wasn't looking anywhere but at Kaine. The other two, that blabbermouth Denton and Kaine's sister, were looking in the window of the music store next to the restaurant.

He narrowed his eyes as he stared at the guide dog walking beside the blind man. Frowning, he stroked the deep vertical line that edged one side of his mouth. That dog could be a problem. He might have to take care of the dog first.

He watched the four of them, laughing and horsing around like a bunch of kids as they got into Denton's T-bird and pulled away from the curb.

Kaine was all lit up tonight, a stupid grin plastered all over his face. If he wasn't such a Sunday do-gooder, a body might think he'd lifted a few.

His mouth curled into a contemptuous smile. It was the woman; that's why Kaine was glowing like a Christmas tree. He had been watching them for over two weeks now. They were almost always together. Sometimes they'd go to her house and eat, then she'd take him up the hill to his place. They went to Como's restaurant a lot, too. Sure, Kaine could afford that. He had to be loaded, the way he was always throwing his money around.

Yeah, they were getting real thick. He'd been watching. He liked to watch the woman. She almost always closed her drapes over the sheer curtains in her living room, but there was enough of a gap at the side of the window that he could still see in. When Kaine wasn't there, she'd curl up on the couch with a pencil tucked behind her ear and read or listen to music.

She was a pretty woman. Too good-looking for a man who couldn't even see her. She had a nice voice, too. Sometimes he listened to her on the radio. But once in a while Kaine would be on the air with her, and then he'd turn them off. He wouldn't listen to them talk to each other on the radio. You could hear her get all smiley when they were together. You could hear in her voice that she liked that big hairy ape.

It didn't matter. Kaine wasn't going to be around much longer. As soon as he tormented him some more, made him pay for the misery he'd brought on him, he'd turn him off for good.

The thought made him snicker out loud. He waited a minute, then pulled out and followed the Thunderbird, staying well behind.

Just as he had hoped, they went to the Terry woman's house. He slowed down almost to a stop and watched as Denton let Kaine and the woman out, then took off with Kaine's sister.

Good. That meant he'd have time to pay a visit to the blind man's empty house.

He pressed the gas pedal a little harder and took off. He felt anxious and excited. With a chuckle of elation, he reached into the deep pocket of his hunting jacket, removed a small flask, and took a quick swig of its contents. After two more gulps he stuck the flask back in his pocket. That was better. He felt warmer now. Ready to deliver his little surprise to the Kaine residence.

He wiped his mouth with the back of one hand, glancing down at the floor on the passenger's side of the truck. His anticipation flared as he looked at the gallon bucket and the crowbar lying beside it.

You like games, Kaine. You been playing games with me for a long time, making me wait, worrying me half-crazy . . . now I'm gonna have the fun. It's my game now, blind man. And you're gonna be the loser.

A sudden unpleasant thought sliced through the thick haze of his mind, causing his laughter to die abruptly. *The woman . . . what if Kaine has told the woman?*

The two were always together. All you had to do was watch them and you could see they had something going. Kaine had kept quiet all these years — probably just biding his time, planning to ruin him eventually — but he hadn't had a girlfriend until now. Wouldn't he likely tell his woman?

The slight tremor in his hands turned to an almost violent shake as he fought to keep a grip on the steering wheel. He began to nod his head up and down, pulling his mouth into a furious snarl. *Maybe he's already told her . . . maybe she already knows.*

He didn't want to hurt the woman. Not yet. He had plans for her, once Kaine was out of the way. Still, he ought to find out what she knew, if anything.

He glanced down once more at the floor of the truck before turning up the hill to Kaine's place. He'd make his little delivery, then go back down to the woman's house and see what he could find out.

He had eavesdropped on them before. Standing outside by the living-room window, he could hear them pretty well. That's what he'd do. There was time. Plenty of time. This was his game now. He'd call the plays.

He smiled. And he'd name the players. The woman was just another part of the game, after all.

NINE

Dan set his empty pie plate on the table beside the couch. Then he stretched, locked his hands behind his head, and leaned comfortably back against the plump cushion, smiling with obvious contentment.

"Well, Jennifer, your banana cream pie more than makes up for your coffee," he said lazily.

Jennifer returned from the kitchen with a fresh cup of coffee for herself and a second glass of milk for him. "I think you should know, Daniel, that no one else has ever complained about my coffee."

He continued to smile, and her heart turned over. It occurred to her that Dan always looked larger in her tiny living room. It also occurred to her that he looked entirely too handsome in that ivory silk shirt.

"Your mustache is white," she told him dryly as he took a big gulp of milk.

Sunny stirred restlessly, raising her head to glance at them, then around the room. Dan stroked her ears, and she soon settled down again. "Have you noticed how much more relaxed Sunny has been tonight?" Jennifer asked. "I think she's finally getting used to the house. Remember how restless she was last week when you had dinner here?"

He nodded. "A lot of things affect her. Even the weather. She's probably hoping for a reward if she's especially good tonight. Like her own piece of banana cream pie, maybe."

"And she just may get it, too. By the way, Daniel," she said with exaggerated emphasis, sitting down beside him. "I read the article in this morning's paper about the award you're getting. I can't believe you didn't tell anyone about it before now."

The local paper had carried a front page announcement that a well-known national organization would be presenting their annual humanitarian award to Dan in recognition of his continuing efforts for the disabled, specifically his work with Helping Hand Farm and the Friend-to-Friend Association.

He shrugged and set his glass down by his plate, dabbing the milk from his mustache with his napkin.

"You're going to be a folk hero if you get any more awards, Daniel," Jennifer teased, thinking of the impressive array of plaques and medallions already decorating his office.

He smiled a little. "It seems to me that the real heroes are the ones who don't get any awards." He rolled up the sleeves of his shirt, then leaned over to give Sunny a pat on the head.

"Dan, you deserve that award," Jennifer protested.

"The ones who really deserve the awards," he went on as if he hadn't heard her, "are the families and friends of the disabled. Sometimes it's even tougher on them than it is on us, but I'm not so sure anyone realizes what *they* go through."

Jennifer collected their dishes and took them into the kitchen, watching him across the counter as she loaded the dishwasher.

"When something happens — like what happened to me," he went on, "we get so caught up in *surviving* that we're often too absorbed in ourselves to realize what's happening in the lives of the people who love us.

"We become so involved in the rehabilitation that we tend to lose touch with what our families are going through. To some extent, we can vent our frustration in the process of rebuilding our lives. But the ones who have to stand by us . . ." His voice drifted, and he waited until Jennifer returned and sat down next to him before going on.

Finally, he leaned forward and rested his elbows on his knees, lacing his fingers together. "I know my family — and Gabe, too — have kept as much of their own pain away from me as possible." His smile was touched with sadness. "But they've suffered right along with me. A lot."

"Your family," Jennifer said sincerely, "is nothing short of wonderful."

"They are, aren't they?" Dan agreed, his tone distracted. Jennifer knew he was remembering.

He remembered that the first sound he had heard, waking up from the nightmare to an even worse reality, had been his mother's soft weeping from across the room. Once she realized he was awake, though, the sobbing had stopped. There had been only her cool hand brushing his hair away from his forehead as she attempted to give him what was left of her own strength. Even now Dan could feel her soft, fragrant cheek pressed against his, as though she could somehow absorb a part of his pain into herself.

And his dad . . . kneeling by the hospital bed, gripping Dan's hand, holding onto him as he prayed unceasingly. Those skillful, highly trained physician's hands that for years had strived to heal the pain and illnesses of others had suddenly been helpless to heal the agony of his only son. Even so, his father had forced him to fight, to reject self-pity and discouragement, in favor of sheer grit and determination. Lucas Kaine had shed his tears alone, so his son need not be wounded even more by his grief.

Lyss had been there, too, of course. Dan could still remember lying there, listening to her pace back and forth in her long-legged, smooth, athletic stride. The soft scent of the baby powder she always used had been strangely comforting in its familiar freshness. Sweet Lyss, trying to be so strong and cheerful and encouraging . . . never letting on how desperately frightened she was for her big brother.

And Gabe . . . faithful friend and brother of his heart. Gabe, who for years had made the story of David and Jonathan come alive for Dan. It had been Gabe who had restrained Dan and made him face what he was doing to those who loved him that awful day — or was it night — when he learned the final verdict, the sentence that had threatened to destroy his hope . . . and his sanity. . . .

He had reached up to push Gabe away, out of his life, along with everyone else. But then he felt the dampness of his friend's tears, and finally they had wept together for Dan's loss. . . .

"Dan?" Jennifer reached out to touch his

shoulder, then hesitated.

He lifted his face, and slowly his features cleared. "Sorry." He smiled, a smile again tinged with sorrow. "I was thinking about heroes."

He slipped his arm around Jennifer's shoulders, and she leaned back against him, thinking how quickly she had grown to feel comfortable and strangely secure with this big, gentle man.

"Tell me about your family, Jennifer," he said casually.

After a moment's hesitation, Jennifer began to speak of her father and her brothers. She told him about Paul first, who at twenty-four had a new wife and a new job as a park ranger. "To Paul, there's nothing worse than a city apartment or a crowded room," she said, smiling. "He would make a wonderful hermit."

Her tone sobered as she told him about Loren, just recently turned nineteen. A victim of cerebral palsy, Jennifer's younger brother spent his days in a wheelchair. "Loren is so special," she said softly. "I don't think he has ever been bored, not once. He has this incredible thirst for learning. He would be — he could have been — a marvelous teacher."

She let her words trail off, then shifted her

attention back to Dan. "He and Dad want to meet you. They're both *very* impressed that I'm working for an Olympic star."

"Your dad must be a pretty impressive guy himself," Dan commented. "The last few years couldn't have been easy for him — without your mother."

"Actually," Jennifer replied, tilting her head so she could look up at him, "Dad is a lot like you."

"Oh? Is that good or bad?"

Jennifer studied his face, then replied as truthfully as she could. "Dad is . . . very strong. Nothing shakes him. He simply — copes. He's a rock." She sighed deeply. "He loves people, too — like you. Dad always finds the best in everyone, and he never seems to take time for his own concerns because he's too busy helping everybody else with theirs."

She was surprised to see that Dan appeared strangely flustered by her words. His voice was almost gruff. "Thank you, Jennifer."

"For what?"

"For comparing me with a man like that." He turned his face away slightly, but not before Jennifer saw a shadow pass across his features. "I'm afraid," he added quietly, "your observation isn't all that accurate. But

I'm still flattered."

Neither of them spoke for several minutes. Finally Dan broke the silence. "Your mother died of cancer, you told me?"

"Yes," Jennifer replied tightly. "When I was sixteen."

His hand tightened on her shoulder, and he rubbed his chin lightly across the top of her head. "That must have been tough for all of you. Was she ill a long time?"

"Two years."

He nodded. "You've had a lot of pain in your life already."

Surprised, Jennifer looked up at him. "Nothing compared to the pain *you've* had."

"Pain is pain, Jennifer," he said gently. "When you lose something or someone precious to you, it leaves a hole in your life."

A hole in her life. That's exactly how Jennifer felt sometimes. As if somewhere, deep inside her spirit, there was a huge, gaping vacuum. An emptiness.

Dan pulled her a little closer. "Jennifer . . . tell me why you won't sing anymore."

"I can't," Jennifer said without explanation.

"Can't — or *won't?*" he parried quietly.

"Is this a counseling session, Daniel?" Jennifer's tone was sharper than she'd intended.

"Not unless you want it to be," he replied

agreeably, squeezing her shoulder. "I think I know a little about what it's like. It feels as though there's a *deadness* inside of you. Like there's nothing where the music used to be except a kind of — silence."

Jennifer stiffened at his incredibly incisive perception, then slumped her shoulders. "Yes," she whispered, not trusting herself to say more.

"I understand that."

She squeezed her eyes shut in response to the note of tenderness in his voice.

"I know that emptiness, Jennifer," he went on, his tone infinitely gentle. "The 'vacuum of despair,' it's called. I suppose I could describe in detail how you feel. But I can also tell you that it doesn't have to last forever."

His fingers lifted a strand of her hair as he went on, obviously choosing his words with a great deal of care.

"Losing hurts. And so we grieve. There's nothing wrong with that. We *need* to grieve. Grief is a vital part of being healed. It doesn't pay to try to shortcut the process. You have to just . . . go through it, experience it, be engulfed by it. At least for a time."

His arm around her tightened protectively. "But sooner or later you have to face the pain. You have to admit that you can't handle it alone. At that point, you have only two real choices. You can accept the circumstance, whatever it is, and lay it down at the feet of the Lord. To do that, you have to believe that God has a reason for allowing even suffering. Whatever the pain, you can be sure that God will work in and through it for your good — and for his glory."

His voice grew even quieter. "Or, you can fight it. You can throw your spiritual fists up and refuse to surrender. If you choose to fight —" he hesitated a fraction of a second, then continued — "you leave that hole in your heart unhealed, and it just keeps getting bigger. The emptiness keeps on growing until it finally swallows you up, until your entire life is absorbed into that gaping, empty abyss . . . and there's nothing left except pain and anger and misery."

"I *have* accepted it," Jennifer murmured dully. "I'm not fighting . . . not anymore."

He sighed deeply as he reached to tip her chin up toward his face. "I don't think so, Jennifer. I think what you've done is *resign* yourself. There's a difference — a critical difference — between resignation and acceptance." He held her tightly, but with exquisite tenderness.

"Resignation doesn't leave any room for hope or joy," he said. "It's a closed door.

141

And sometimes a lot of anger and resentment are trapped behind that door. But acceptance leaves the door open for God to work his will." He paused for a long moment, then added, "What I hear in your voice, Jennifer, is *resignation.*"

As though anticipating her protest, he stopped her words by gently touching a finger to her lips. "When we're children, trust comes naturally to us. We accept — because we still see God as a loving Father. But when we grow up, well, we seem to find resignation easier than acceptance.

"We grow older, and we learn about things like cancer and war and famine and AIDS. Sometimes we start to think that God has changed, and we lose our hope, or we assume he was never what we believed him to be in the first place — and we lose our trust. As our world gets bigger and wider, we discover that a lot of it is ugly and filled with injustice and pain. But what we forget," he said, his voice dropping until it was scarcely more than a whisper, "is that the God of our childhood is still bigger than the world and all the suffering it can bring us."

He coaxed her head against his chest and held her for a long time. Jennifer somehow sensed that Dan had just thrown her a lifeline — if only she could make herself grab hold of it. She heard the truth and the wisdom of his words. But she wasn't anything like Dan. What was easy for him might well be impossible for her.

In contrast to his maturity, strength, and wisdom, she was full of confusion and bitterness and rebellion. Regrettably, she feared that no amount of understanding or caring or even love could ever close the gap between them.

As if he could sense the turmoil going on inside her, Dan put her gently away from him for a moment and pulled something out of his shirt pocket. "Here — I brought you something."

Jennifer looked at him.

He pressed an unlabeled cassette tape into her hand. "It's the demo for *Daybreak*. I thought you might want to listen to it. Sorry I don't have a book — all I had at home was my Braille score." He paused a beat and said quietly but pointedly, "You just say the word, and I'll get a book for you."

"Dan, please don't —"

"I want you to listen to the tape," he insisted. "That's all. The music — and the lyrics — are special to me." His smile made something warm and infinitely tender wrap itself around Jennifer's aching heart. "All I'm trying to do is share something that's special to me with someone . . . who's also very special to me."

Jennifer took the tape.

Abruptly, Dan stood and pulled her to her feet. As if to shift the mood to a more comfortable lightness, he informed her he was now ready for his second piece of pie. "Before old Gabe shows up and does me out of it."

"Right, boss," Jennifer agreed, grateful for the change in mood.

They headed for the kitchen, with Sunny padding along behind them. "I suppose you want another glass of —"

Jennifer stopped dead as she saw the face staring in the window of the back door. Dan crashed solidly into her from behind, the sudden thrust of his weight nearly knocking her off balance.

"Whoa! Your turn signal's out, lady!" he said, laughing as he caught her shoulders with both hands.

At the same time, Sunny muttered a low growl and charged the rest of the way into the kitchen. She hit the back door full force, barking and snarling, looking back at Dan as if to reassure herself that he was safe.

"Daniel . . ." Jennifer's throat felt like sandpaper. An icy rope of fear snaked the entire length of her body.

Dan stood unmoving, obviously tense. "What's wrong?"

The skull-like face at the window was gone. He had turned to flee as soon as he'd seen Jennifer approaching. But she was still unable to move, riveted in place by the memory of that spectral face peering in at them.

"Jennifer?" Dan pressed more insistently. "What is it?"

"Daniel, someone was out there — watching us."

Dan tightened his hold on her shoulders. "What do you mean? Where?" His voice was suddenly rough.

"Outside — at the kitchen door. He ran as soon as he saw me." Jennifer's voice was trembling as violently as her hands.

Dan heard the tremor in her voice, even above the din Sunny was making. He silenced the retriever with an abrupt command, calling her to his side. He stood unmoving, holding Jennifer to him as he tried to think.

After a moment, she slipped out of his grasp. "I'm going to look out the side window," she whispered.

"Be careful," Dan cautioned her, feeling a wave of anger and frustration rise at his own helplessness. "Do you see anything?"

"No, nothing. I'm sure he's gone. I probably scared him as much as he scared me," Jennifer said, her voice still unsteady.

"What's Sunny doing? Is she still watching the door?"

"No. She's watching you."

Dan gave a nod. "Then he must be gone. But stay away from the door. And turn out the lights." He hesitated. "If there are any curtains or drapes open, close them."

Dan listened to her moving around in the living room, flipping switches and drawing drapes. The sound he was waiting for came within seconds — the familiar sound of a pickup truck pulling away. His stomach knotted when he heard the faint rattle and the recognizable miss as the noise of the motor faded into the night.

Jennifer returned, touching his shoulder. He wrapped an arm around her. "This just infuriates me," she grumbled. "I haven't had a Peeping Tom since I was in college. You'd think —" She stopped suddenly. "Dan — what's wrong? You're pale as a ghost!"

Instinctively, Dan gathered Jennifer even more tightly against him.

"Dan? What is it?"

Dan's mind was reeling. *It had to be the same truck . . . the same man.* The realization

146

chilled him. Had the man been watching *him* . . . or Jennifer?

Guilt stabbed at him as he realized that his silence about the phone calls and threats might have endangered her. If his obsession about his precious independence had jeopardized Jennifer in any way, he would never be able to forgive himself.

"Daniel —"

"It's all right — he's gone."

"Yes, I heard the car leave, too, but why —"

"It's not a car, it's a truck."

"Oh — you can tell just by hearing the engine? I don't know how you —"

"It's the same truck that ran us off the road," he said shortly.

"Are you sure?" She sounded skeptical.

"I'm sure," he said, not explaining. "You can turn on the lights now. And call Gabe. Then we'll call the police."

"The police?"

Dan heard the confusion in her voice. "He could come back," he said. "Just . . . call Gabe, would you? I'd like him to be here when the police come. He'll still be at Lyss's apartment. Have him bring her, too. You can go back to her place to spend the night."

"No, I don't need to do that —"

"Jennifer — would you just do what I ask!"

He felt her tense at his sharpness, and he quickly gentled his tone. "Please. I'll explain later."

Silently, she moved out of his embrace and made the calls.

TEN

Gabe and Lyss were no more than three or four minutes ahead of the police.

Within minutes, both officers had come back inside from checking the area to report they had found nothing except some footprints and tire tracks.

"You were right, Miss Terry," said the taller of the two policemen. "Apparently, he'd been standing close to the front window, as well as on the back porch. You can track him through the snow."

Jennifer offered coffee to both officers, and they drank it in the living room while Dan gave them an accounting of his anonymous phone calls and the incidents with the pickup truck. He also revealed his suspicion that someone had been watching his house at night — probably the same man Jennifer had seen at the kitchen door. He kept to himself — for the moment at least — his hunch about a possible connection between the harassment and the upcoming radiothon. Nor did he reveal the depth of rage and sick hatred he had sensed in his tormentor.

When he had finished his tale, he waited. Even though he couldn't see their faces, he sensed that Gabe and Lyss — and probably

Jennifer — were more than a little upset with him.

Lyss wasted no time in confirming his assumption. "I can't *believe* you've kept all this to yourself, Dan! *Why?*"

Jennifer was quick to jump in with her two cents worth. "Dan, how *could* you? You could have been hurt — or even worse — and none of us would have even known you were in danger!"

Surprisingly, Gabe waited until the women had vented their outrage before pointing out to Dan that he should have at least told *him*. "I have been known, on occasion, to keep my mouth shut if it's absolutely necessary, you know. This wasn't one of your brighter moves, pal."

Dan nodded his agreement to every charge they hurled at him, making no attempt to defend himself. "If you're all finished, I think the officers have a few questions they want to ask me," he said quietly.

An embarrassed hush fell over the room as Lyss and Jennifer muttered hasty apologies.

"Dan, do you have *any* idea who might be doing this?" asked Rick Hill, one of the policemen.

Dan pushed his hands down into his pockets and shook his head. "No, I don't, Rick.

It could be anyone." Hesitating, he made a quick decision, then added, "But I've got a hunch the radiothon may be yanking this fellow's chain."

"Why do you think that, sir?" asked the other officer, a rookie Dan hadn't met before tonight.

"Because the phone calls and all the rest of it started when we first began to advertise the radiothon on the air," Dan explained. "He's made several cracks about me 'minding my own business' or 'sticking my nose in where I don't belong.' "

Neither policeman spoke for a few seconds. Finally, Rick Hill began to question Jennifer. "Miss Terry? Is there a man who might be upset with you or Dan? An ex-boyfriend, maybe?"

Dan heard the puzzlement in Jennifer's voice. "There's no one like that," she said. "Besides, as I told you, I didn't recognize the man I saw at the door."

Again she described the face she had seen, shuddering at the memory. "I think he was middle-aged — or older. Very thin . . . extremely thin. He looked almost —"

When she stopped, the younger of the two officers gently prompted her. "Yes, ma'am?"

"It sounds ridiculous," Jennifer went on, "but he had a face like a — a corpse. Bony,

151

sunken — and very pale."

Dan heard the policeman's pen scrape the paper as he made a note of her words. "Well, there's not a whole lot we can do tonight," said Rick Hill. "But one thing's for sure, Dan — you shouldn't be by yourself until we find out what's going on. You're entirely too —" He let his sentence drift off, obviously feeling awkward.

"Helpless?" Dan supplied, with a slight lift of his chin.

"Well — not that, but certainly . . . vulnerable."

"He won't be alone," Gabe said flatly.

Dan jerked his head in Gabe's direction, a sharp retort on his tongue. Instead, he bit back his protest and said nothing.

It was starting, just as he had known it would.

As they all made ready to leave, Dan was surprised when Jennifer drew him into the kitchen. "Dan," she said, holding tightly to his arm, "I want you to know . . . if I seemed angry a few minutes ago, I wasn't. It's just that I'm so afraid for you. And I hate it that you've been going through all this alone."

Before Dan could reply, she added, "What I'm trying to say is that, even though I wish you'd told us, I think I understand why you didn't."

A wave of gratitude, almost painful in its sweet intensity, swelled deep inside Dan. Jennifer tightened her grasp on his arm as she went on. "I think I know what your freedom — your independence — means to you, Dan." Her voice sounded small and unsteady. "I also know that the only reason you finally told us the truth is because you were concerned for *me*. Please promise me you'll let Gabe stay with you until this is over. I need to know you won't be alone."

Dan nodded in resignation. Somehow, the realization that she understood made everything a little easier, a little more bearable. But that shouldn't surprise him. Jennifer had her own special way of making everything she touched just a little bit better . . . at least for him.

ELEVEN

"Gabe — I want your word that you won't say anything about this yet to my folks."

The two of them were sitting at the counter in Dan's kitchen, drinking coffee and talking. It was almost eleven, but Dan was too tense to sleep, and he could tell by Gabe's voice that his friend's nerves were stretched as tightly as his own.

Gabe uttered a small grunt of skepticism. "You don't really think Lyss is going to keep quiet about this, do you?"

"She will," Dan said meaningfully, "if you ask her to and explain why you agree with me."

"Buddy, you overestimate my influence with your sister," Gabe grumbled. "But I'll give it a try. I'd better call her yet tonight before she has a chance to get on the phone with your mother."

Dan nodded with relief. "While you talk to Lyss, I'm going to do a few laps. I've got to loosen up if I'm going to get any sleep." He stood and walked across the kitchen to the door that opened into the pool area. "Come on in and join me when you get off the phone."

Gabe's voice was laced with exaggerated

disgust. "You know I believe in total sloth after seven P.M. No, you run along and play, Daniel. I'll talk to the lovely Alyssa and then take Sunny outside for her bedtime thing. Maybe by then you'll have come to your senses."

Dan grinned and shook his head, then went on to the pool, flipping on the light in case Gabe decided to follow after all. For a moment, he thought he caught a whiff of an unfamiliar odor. He frowned, shrugged, then went on to the small dressing room on the east wall and changed.

He dove into the pool quickly, plunging himself immediately under the water. He was eager for the quiet comfort, the soothing blanket of calm that he knew would soon wash over him.

But something was wrong. A slight difference in the rhythm of the water, a barely discernible sluggishness, made him suspect a problem with the filtering system. Curious, he surfaced and gasped for air.

The strange, unfamiliar smell he had noticed on entering the pool area assaulted him full force. At the same time, he felt a thick, sticky mass thread its way down his face and begin to spread over his shoulders. He shook his head violently back and forth in an attempt to throw off whatever it was.

When it didn't budge, he treaded water and began to pull his fingers through his hair and over his beard. The stuff was like liquid glue. He turned a few inches in the water, and when he did, the same viscous muck slapped relentlessly at his upper arms and torso.

For the first time in his life, Dan panicked in the water. An unholy dread assailed him, and his heart seemed to stop. In desperation he scissored himself and plunged beneath the water, trying to wash away the revolting substance from his body. But when he broke above the water again, he knew instantly he had done himself no good. The stuff was like tentacles, and there seemed to be no shaking it.

He fought to put down the paralyzing grip of panic. He forced himself to swim, shouting wildly for Gabe as he hurtled through the water.

At the side of the pool, he struggled to pull himself out of the water. He heard Gabe cry out and at the same time slipped and lost his balance. Totally disoriented now, he groped wildly for something to hang onto. He cracked his elbow, then hit his head on the wall of the pool before Gabe was finally able to grasp him firmly under the arms and haul him out of the water.

The room suddenly became a surreal chamber of Gabe's shouts and Dan's labored gasps for air. He felt himself losing consciousness and wondered if he was going to die. Gabe was gripping his shoulders so hard that pain shot down his back. Lights flashed on and off in his head. The smell grew stronger.

Gabe sounded furious, desperate. "Dan! *Dan!* Can you hear me? It's all right, buddy, it's all right . . . it's only paint . . . it's red paint, man, that's all . . . just paint."

Gabe kept yelling at him, crying his name. He was panicky, too. Dan could hear it in his voice.

"I thought it was blood. . . . I heard you shout and I saw you coming up out of that water . . . covered with that red mess. I thought it was blood . . . I thought you were bleeding . . . I thought you were dying, man!"

Dan finally caught a breath, then slumped in Gabe's arms.

Humiliation was no stranger to Dan. In five years of being blind, he had suffered his share of indignities and had survived any number of embarrassing moments. He had handled most of them without completely losing his sense of humor.

He reminded himself that no one but his best friend had witnessed the scene in the swimming pool. But for some reason he still felt like a fool.

He sat on a chair in the large bathroom off the pool, docilely allowing Gabe to wash paint off him. The entire bathroom — especially himself, he thought with a disgusted sniff — reeked of turpentine.

He was aware that Gabe was doing his best to snap him out of his black mood. "Don't get within ten feet of an open flame for the next few days, buddy. You don't want to be responsible for the big boom all on your own."

When Dan made no reply, Gabe tried a different tack. "Does Jennifer like your beard?"

"What?"

"Your beard, man. Does she like it?"

"How do I know if she —" Dan thought for a moment, then sighed. "She's never complained about it."

"So you'd like it saved, I suppose."

"Saved?"

"It would be easier if the beard went," Gabe said carefully. "Along with an inch or two of your hair, my friend."

Dan made no attempt to match Gabe's humor. "I've had a beard ever since the accident. It's a lot easier than shaving in the dark."

"Right," Gabe said quickly. "We'll just soak it in turpentine."

Neither made any further attempt at conversation for a long time. Finally, as if he were unable to stand the silence any longer, Gabe said, "You all right, buddy?"

"I'm fine," Dan answered wearily. "Just tired."

"The police are coming out again first thing in the morning," Gabe told him.

"Why? They weren't able to find anything when they were here tonight."

"It won't hurt to check around again when it's daylight. The guy might have dropped something they missed in the dark."

"Did he break the pool-house door when he jimmied it?" Dan asked.

"No. The lock is sprung, but the door wasn't even splintered. We'll get a deadbolt put on there tomorrow."

"I'm glad Jennifer went home with Lyss. I'm worried sick that this nut will try something with her." Dan's pulse hammered at the thought.

"I still can't believe he pulled a stunt like this," Gabe grated out. "I'm telling you, Dan, we've got to watch you every minute until they catch this guy. He's a real sicko."

"Nobody's going to watch me every *minute!*"
Dan spat furiously. "I had enough of that
before!"

Gabe halted his ministration to Dan's
face. "I know," he said quietly. "But the
alternative could be a lot worse. Dan, this
is no practical joker we're dealing with here.
Someone out there wants your skin. Who-
ever he is, whatever his reasons, he's out to
get you. This guy is a *nut case,* Dan!"

Dan swallowed hard and slumped a little
lower in the chair. "It's Jennifer I'm worried
about."

"Well, that balances out, old buddy,"
Gabe said lightly. "Because it's *you* Jennifer's
worried about. As for me, I'd kinda like to
lock both of you up for a while."

The nightmare came again that night. Dan
fought it, as always, sensing even in the labyrinth of his subconscious that this time might
be the time he didn't survive the terror. But
it burrowed through his defenses, through
the tunnel of his sleep, just as the headlights
had cut through the mountains that foggy
night. . . .

*He felt the car bumping and weaving on the
narrow, potholed road . . . heard the soft background music of the radio, turned to his own
station . . . smelled the new-leather scent of the*

Buick . . . tasted the dank humidity of the night. He even saw his own eyes in the rearview mirror as he lightly tapped his fingers on the steering wheel in time to the music. . . .

But this time the nightmare didn't end as it usually did. This time there was something different about it. It went on, past the headlights and the deafening crunch of metal and his own scream of terrified denial. A flash of color suddenly zigzagged in front of him, a spray of red and black —

And then it was over, and he was awake. He sat bolt upright in bed, drenched in perspiration and gripped by a new, almost irrational fear. Tonight he felt more terrorized than ever before. He could have screamed with his desperation to banish the horror from his mind once and for all.

Instead, he faced the sickening, inescapable conviction that it would simply go on and on, through countless nights of his life, until he finally discovered whatever it was that waited for him at the end.

At least he hadn't wakened screaming this time. He expelled a shaky breath and kicked the blankets off, then got up and made his way to the bathroom to splash cold water on his face. Sunny padded quietly along behind him, waited, then returned to the bedroom with him — as though she, too, sensed the need to watch over him more cautiously than ever.

His head was still pounding. He figured his blood pressure must peak at stroke level every time he had the nightmare, and tonight had been even worse.

For a long time, he sat on the side of the bed and rested his head on his hands, thinking . . . and finally praying. . . .

Oh, Lord, please forgive me for my selfishness of these past weeks, for staying silent about the phone calls and everything else. I know it was nothing but pride. Lord, help me to get past this stubborn need to handle everything on my own. Just look at what I've done. . . . If Jennifer had been hurt, I think I'd die, Lord. I couldn't live with knowing I'd hurt her by my own foolish pride. . . .

After a while he stretched out on the bed, reached to give Sunny a reassuring pat, and then lay, eyes open, for another hour or more. Occasionally he thought about Jennifer and managed to smile. Once he wept. Finally, he fell into a restless, troubled sleep.

TWELVE

Jennifer spent the next few days in an agony of suspense and dread, but the time was surprisingly uneventful. Even the phone calls to Dan had stopped. No more uninvited visitors at her bungalow, no more hair-raising attacks by the pickup truck, no more terrorizing pranks like the episode in Dan's swimming pool. Unfortunately, no new leads had developed in the police investigation either.

Dan had had a professional service drain, clean, and refill the pool. It had taken most of the week. By Sunday, Jennifer's routine had also returned to normal. She could almost relax and pretend that everything was as it should be. But there was no denying the undercurrent of foreboding that never quite went away. Dan had revealed enough about *his* suspicions to trigger her own anxiety, and she lived with an underlying apprehension that affected her every waking hour.

Her enthusiasm for the radiothon had ebbed, the initial excitement changing to dread. She had suggested to Dan that he cancel, or at least postpone, the whole event. But she might as well have saved her breath. A stubborn thrust of his chin and a firm shake of his head were his only reply.

He was obviously determined to go through with the radiothon, and that was that. The best they could hope for was that the police would soon turn up a clue that would lead to the end of this sick campaign of terror.

Jennifer could scarcely bear to think about the incident with the paint in Dan's swimming pool. He finally seemed to be snapping out of the despondency that had settled over him after that awful night. But this cruel wave of torment was taking its toll on him. His step lacked its usual spring these days. His smile faded a little more quickly, and his voice held a note of hesitancy that hadn't been there before. It was as though small pieces of his confidence were being hacked away, one chip at a time. He seemed to have to work much harder these days at maintaining his sense of humor. Still, he managed to surprise her in the most unexpected ways.

Like this afternoon's phone call.

"*Sledding?* No, Daniel, I am not coming up to go sledding with you and Jason. I am *tired.* Can you say *tired,* Daniel?"

Jennifer shifted the telephone receiver to her other ear as she edged the kitchen curtains back to look outside. An unexpected spring snowfall brightened the late afternoon gloom. It *was* beautiful. . . .

But, no. Definitely not. She was going to bed early tonight, just as she had been promising herself for several days now.

"You may function very well on nothing but adrenaline," she said to Dan, "but we weaker mortals need something called *sleep*."

She could almost believe the apologetic note in his voice was genuine when he answered. "I'm really sorry, Jennifer. I *have* kept you too busy the last few days, haven't I?"

"You might say that," Jennifer agreed dryly.

"I understand. I'll explain to the boys. Jim Arbegunst is here, too, so he can help Jason with his sled. Mom will be disappointed, though. She wanted us to come to dinner afterward. Pork roast and dressing." He paused, then added, "And fudge cake."

Jennifer glanced down woefully at her half-eaten peanut butter and pickle sandwich — her Sunday dinner. "That's bribery, Daniel."

"It is, isn't it?" he admitted cheerfully.

"Well," she waffled. "I'd have to eat and run. Your mother might be offended." With a frown of distaste, she dropped the remainder of her sandwich into the trash can by the refrigerator.

"She knows how swamped we are," Dan put in. "She'd probably even send some dessert home with you, if you couldn't stay."

"You think?"

"I'll see to it. You'll come, then?"

"I suppose. But I *am* leaving early, Daniel."

"Oh, absolutely."

Suddenly another thought occurred to Jennifer. "What about Gabe? He *is* still staying with you at night, isn't he?"

"Not tonight. He drove over to Clarksburg to cover the concert at First Baptist, remember?"

"*Dan* — you promised you wouldn't stay alone at night until —"

"It's already taken care of." Jennifer heard the forced patience in his tone. "That's why Jim is here. He's staying over tonight."

"Jim is only a teenager, Daniel —"

"Jim is nearly six feet tall," Dan pointed out, "and perfectly capable of providing exactly what I need — a person in the house who can see what I can't."

Jennifer didn't like it. But he had used his "don't push me" tone of voice. And maybe he was right, after all. The important thing was that he have someone in the house with him who could see.

Not that he seemed to require a lot of assistance. Jennifer didn't even stop to wonder how Dan would manage sledding.

Radar, how else? she thought with a wry smile, slipping into a pair of thermal underwear and her oldest jeans.

Dan and the boys were already outside when Jennifer pulled into the driveway. Jason, out of breath with excitement, met her at the car.

"Are you going to ride on my sled, Jennifer?"

Jennifer rumpled his hair and, taking his hand, walked with him up the driveway toward Dan and Jim. "Is that shiny red sled yours, Jason?"

His head bobbed up and down. "Dan gave it to me for Christmas!"

"Well, since red is one of my favorite colors," Jennifer said, grinning at him, "I am definitely going to ride on your sled."

She walked up to Dan and gave his hand a quick squeeze. "Is it dinnertime yet?"

He shot her a cryptic smile as he zipped up his gray snowmobile jacket. "You have to earn your dinner, Jennifer."

Jennifer glanced warily from Sunny — who was off her harness and obviously ready for fun — to Jason. "Oh, no," she groaned. "This looks suspiciously like a three-on-a-sled deal to me!"

Dan's arm went around her shoulders

167

companionably. "You catch on fast."

Jennifer turned to Jim. "Why do I get myself into these situations?"

The boy turned his haunted eyes on Jennifer, as if infinitely grateful for her attention. "Don't worry, Miss Terry. I'll take Jason and Sunny with me."

"You're a brave boy, Jim," Dan said with a chuckle. "And I'm not even going to argue with you. All right, gang, let's get going!"

"You're really going to ride with me?" Dan pulled their sled with one hand as Jennifer took his other arm. Sunny had already bolted ahead with the boys.

"Only if you promise no belly-whoppin'," Jennifer warned him.

"Well . . . it might be better if you steer," he suggested after a second or two.

"Actually, Daniel, I had already thought of that."

By the time they reached the top of the hill, they met Jim and Jason on their first trip down. Jason was squealing with delight and hanging tightly onto Sunny, who was tucked securely between the two boys.

Jennifer almost gave up before they even got started. Trying to fit on a sled in front of Dan was next to impossible. "You need a two-seater," she ranted, eyeing his long legs hopelessly.

Laughing, Dan enfolded her as tightly as possible inside his arms, tucked his legs precariously outside hers, pulled her snugly back against his chest, and yelled, *"Geronimo!"*

Their first slide down was surprisingly smooth. In fact, by their third downhill run, they agreed they made quite a pair and that there was really nothing to it except skill and lightning-fast reflexes.

But on their fourth trip down, Dan leaned too far to the left, causing them to lose control. Before either of them knew what had happened, they found themselves tumbled together in the middle of an enormous snowdrift.

Jennifer scrambled awkwardly to her knees, staring openmouthed at Dan, who was laughing so hard he choked on a spray of snow.

Rolling onto his side, he caught his breath and molded a sizable snowball, which he proceeded to toss at Jennifer with surprising accuracy.

Jennifer scrambled toward him. Wiping the snow from her face, she began to pummel him with her mittened fists. This only made him collapse into helpless laughter. Finally he hauled himself onto his knees and caught her by the wrists. "Don't you beat on *me*, slugger!" he warned, still laughing.

"*You're* supposed to be the navigator here, remember? I'm just along for the ride."

"Ohhh! Just let me up! Get away, Daniel! I mean it, now! Let me up, I'm going to —"

"You're going to *what?*" he drawled, balancing on his knees. "You're all right, aren't you, hon?" he asked with a phony expression of concern. "Here — I've got something for you."

"What?" Jennifer narrowed her eyes.

"Just open your mouth."

"Daniel Kaine, don't you *dare* —" Her last words got swallowed up by the handful of snow he pushed at her face.

Yanking herself free, Jennifer then let go with a few snowballs of her own. But within seconds, she gave up. Dan, as if sensing her surrender, poised on his knees and smiled a slow, lazy smile, then dipped his head in search of her face. Jennifer ducked, deliberately twisting back and forth so he couldn't find her, then breaking up in laughter at the determined smirk on his face.

"Stop that, woman," he ordered sternly, finally catching her chin in his hand and holding her steady. "You're fouling up my radar." His expression suddenly sobered. He whispered her name as if savoring the sound of it, then covered her mouth very gently with his own.

Something infinitely tender and achingly sweet squeezed Jennifer's heart. She watched him from a soft haze, wondering at the small sigh he uttered as he released her, then brushed her cheek with a fleeting touch of his gloved fingertips.

Both of them remained silent, unmoving, like two statues in the snow, Jennifer searching Dan's face. Slowly, he removed his gloves, tossed them to one side, and framed her face between his hands. He held her gently but firmly for a long moment before touching his lips to her temple. "Jennifer . . . I love you."

THIRTEEN

The incredible power of emotion behind his words made Jennifer lose her breath. She stared up at Dan's love-softened face, involuntarily reaching out a hand to caress his bearded cheek. Her breath, when she finally found it again, was as ragged and uneven as his.

Dan slipped his arms around her and gathered her to him, cradling her against his chest and rocking her slowly back and forth in the snow. Jennifer thought her heart would break and shatter into a thousand pieces when she heard his anguished whisper against her forehead. "Ah, Jennifer . . . what I would give to look at you, to see you — really *see* you — just once."

Those achingly honest words opened her heart and her senses as nothing else could have. All her fears about being wrong for him, all her doubts about being good for him, were swept away for one wonderful, unforgettable moment.

She pulled her gloves off and cupped his face between her hands, pulling his head gently down to her. "Oh, Daniel, you *have* seen me," she murmured just before touching her lips to his. "You've seen my heart."

His hands trembled on her shoulders. "I

know I have the most colossal gall in the world to say this to you. And I may be way out of line, but I have to say it now because I might not ever have the courage again."

Jennifer held her breath, half afraid of what she was about to hear.

He turned her slightly in his arms so he could rest his hands more firmly on her shoulders, keeping her close, yet holding her just far enough away from him that she could see his breath in the cold air. Gone now was his earlier expression of uncertainty and the faltering note of doubt in his voice. Instead he wore a look of decision, the expression of a man who has met his destiny and is about to surrender to it.

"I am head-over-heels, hopelessly in love with you, my sweet rebel." The tenderness that settled over his face caught Jennifer's heart by surprise and held it captive. "I think," Dan added softly, "I was as good as totaled the first day you walked into the station, when I found you stumbling around with your eyes closed so you'd know how it felt to be blind."

He gave a slow nod, and Jennifer saw a fleeting gleam of insight dart across his features. "You've changed my life, love. For the first time in years, I feel like a whole man again. Jennifer . . . I'm asking you . . .

if you'll marry me."

Jennifer could do nothing but stare at him, as limp beneath his hands as a rag doll. She hadn't expected this. Of course she had known he cared for her . . . but *love? Marriage?* Impossible. She was light-years away from this man in every way that mattered.

"I know I can't offer you anything but broken pieces," he was saying quietly, "but I'll love you more than any woman has ever been loved by a man. I can promise you that much, at least."

Jennifer looked at him with dismay. She swallowed, cleared her throat, still unable to face the growing uncertainty now settling over Dan's face. "Dan . . . I don't know. I'm not sure, that is — what to say. . . ."

He smiled, though his voice was unsteady when he answered. "How about something like, 'I can't live without you, Daniel' for starters? I could be content with that. For a while, anyway."

"Oh, Dan — I *do* care for you, but —"

"How much?" His hands tightened on her shoulders.

"What?"

"How much do you care for me?"

"Well, I can't put my feelings into words, exactly. I can't just —"

"Try."

Jennifer gaped at him, her mind suddenly reeling at this whole impossible situation. "Well, I care a *lot,* I suppose, but —"

"Do you love me, Jennifer?"

"Daniel, you don't just answer a question like that in the middle of a snowdrift! Besides — we really haven't known each other long enough to —"

"Do you *love* me, Jennifer?"

He reached for her hands and enfolded them between his own. With an expression of great patience, he waited.

"Now, Daniel . . . you know we're nothing alike. In fact, we're total opposites."

He nodded agreeably.

"Oh, we may have a few things in common," she conceded, "but basically we're like —"

"Oil and water?" he supplied helpfully.

Jennifer blinked. "Well — that may be a bit extreme. But certainly we don't see things the same way at all. You're very patient, and I'm not."

"Mm. That's true."

Jennifer looked at him. "You're very — accepting. And tolerant. And we *both* know I'm not."

He nodded his head sagely. "I'm afraid that's also true."

"Nothing seems to bother you. You're just

a very mellow, easygoing man."

"Granted."

"You're — philosophical. I'm analytical. You're careful and precise. I'm impetuous and completely unorganized. And tense. I'm very tense. I'll probably have ulcers by the time I'm thirty."

"Marry me and have kids instead." He raised both her hands to his lips and skimmed a gentle kiss over her knuckles.

"And we never agree on anything, besides —" Jennifer glanced up at the lazy smile on his face. "What did you say?"

"I think I just proposed again," he said, still smiling.

The soft touch of amusement in his voice faded to a more serious tone. "Tell me something, Jennifer. Does my blindness have anything to do with the way you're evading the question?"

Jennifer gasped, appalled that he could think such a thing about her after all this time. "Of course not!"

As she watched, a subtle look of relief crossed Dan's face. "Forgive me. I had to ask. You, more than anyone else, know the problems that will accompany me into marriage."

"Oh, Daniel," she murmured, the words breaking her heart even as she spoke them.

"It has nothing to do with your being blind! You're — a *wonderful* man! You're sweet, and you're strong, and you're thoughtful — a woman couldn't hope for a finer man than you! But you deserve someone who's . . . more *like* you, not someone like me."

He seemed to wince at her words. "Jennifer . . . my love, I'd do anything to make you see the truth about me." He clasped her hands tightly in his. "Don't you understand, Jennifer? There's nothing special or unique about me! If I were as strong as you think I am, I'd get out of your life today. No, love — I'm just a man, a very ordinary man who wants the same things any other ordinary man wants. All I want," he said, his voice almost a whisper, "is a woman to love, a home to share with her, and maybe some children to call me Daddy."

He hesitated, then asked her again, "Jennifer . . . do you love me?" Jennifer held her breath. She saw his hopeful expression change to a stricken look of defeat. Without quite knowing what she was doing, she moved more closely into his arms. "Yes," she said in a voice so faint it was nearly lost in the wind, "I'm afraid I do."

She looked up into his face then, and she thought the expression of relief and happiness settling over him was the most beautiful sight she had ever seen in her life.

He wrapped her snugly in his arms and whispered against the hollow of her cheek. "Don't be afraid, Jennifer. Don't ever be afraid to love me. I'll never hurt you. Don't you know by now that I'd die before I'd ever hurt you?"

They remained silent for a long moment, locked in each other's embrace.

Jennifer finally broke the silence. "Dan — I *do* love you. But that doesn't mean I'm ready to talk about marriage yet."

"I'm really sorry to hear you say that, Jennifer," he said with mock disapproval, "because if your intentions are anything other than honorable, this relationship will never work."

"Stop that!" she scolded, poking a finger into his chest. "This is very serious, Daniel."

"Uh . . . can I say just one thing, love?"

"What?" she snapped.

"I hear the happy sound of children's laughter. Could we possibly continue this conversation inside, where it's a little warmer and a whole lot more private?"

Startled, Jennifer peered over his shoulder. Sure enough, Jim and Jason and Sunny were barreling over the slope of the hill, only a few feet away from them. "We may be able to manage the warmth by going inside to the fire, Daniel. But privacy?" She shook her head. "Don't count on it."

Later, after everyone had changed into dry clothes and warmed up with hot cocoa, Dan agreed to let the boys use the pool. "But we'll have to leave here no later than five if we don't want to miss dinner. So when I say it's time, you guys will have to move."

Sunny, obviously determined not to miss the fun, squeezed through the door with the two boys as they left the kitchen.

"It's odd how well they get along together, considering the age difference," Jennifer commented. She was sitting on one side of the kitchen counter, noting Dan's easy but precise movements as he placed their cups in the dishwasher and wiped off the sink with a sponge.

"Jim is absolutely starved for attention, for someone to care about him."

Surprised, Jennifer looked at him. "But what about his father?"

Dan gave a sigh and dried his hands. "Jim is a lonely, unhappy boy," he said with a troubled frown. "I'm afraid his father's idea of attention is a strong rod."

Jennifer puzzled over his words, but he didn't explain. Instead, he walked around to her side of the counter and tugged lightly at

179

a damp strand of hair. "So," he said, changing the subject, "have you listened to the tape I gave you yet?"

"No, I haven't listened to the tape you gave me yet," Jennifer retorted glibly. "When exactly do you think I would have had time?"

"I seem to remember you having a cassette deck in your car," he countered. "Why are you putting it off?"

"I'm *not* putting it off."

A knowing smile curved his mouth, but he said nothing.

"I really *haven't* had time, Daniel! And we know whose fault that is."

He shrugged agreeably. "It's just as well, maybe. There's something else I probably should have given you first."

He walked to the large rolltop desk that sat between the dining area and the living room, returning with a loose-leaf notebook.

"What's this?" Jennifer asked as he laid the notebook on the counter in front of her.

"Actually, it's a kind of journal," he said quietly.

Jennifer glanced curiously from him to the notebook. "A journal?"

Dan nodded. "It's something I started not too long after the accident."

He went into the living room and bent

down to stir up the fire. Then he straightened, turning back to her. With his hands in his pockets, he stood, saying nothing as he scuffed the toe of his shoe against the floor.

His attention abruptly shifted back to Jennifer. "I'm sure it'll be hard to read," he said, gesturing to the notebook. "My handwriting was pretty bad even when I could see. Katharine didn't start typing my notes until later."

He lifted his chin, his expression uncertain. "I just thought it might help you with some of the questions you seem to have," he said carefully. "I thought —" He choked off a sound of frustration. "I don't know *what* I thought. I'm sorry, Jennifer, I know I don't have any right to push my opinions onto you." He turned away from her to face the fireplace.

Jennifer stared at his back for a moment, then glanced down at the notebook. She opened it and began to leaf through it, her eyes drawn to the words on the first few dog-eared pages. There seemed to be page after page of Dan's own words, miscellaneous quotes, and Scripture verses, scrawled unevenly but still legible.

Something sad and poignantly tender wafted through her as the significance of what she held in her hands finally registered. Before her were months of Dan's most personal, excruciating agony . . . hundreds of his heartrending, soul-searching thoughts and discoveries. He was opening his deepest, innermost feelings to her.

She got up very slowly and walked to him. When she reached his side, she laid her hand gently on his shoulder and waited for him to face her. "Daniel," she said softly, "are you sure you want me to read this?"

He nodded but didn't answer right away. "Yes. I do," he finally said, his voice quiet. "And not entirely because I'm hoping you'll find something in it — to help you. Some of my reasons are selfish, I admit."

His tone was gentle but steady as he explained. "I think I'm selfish enough to want you to understand what it was like — after the accident — and coward enough not to want to tell you."

Jennifer stared up at him, then shook her head slowly from side to side. "No —" Her voice broke and she hesitated. "I don't think so. I don't believe you have a selfish or cowardly bone in your body, Daniel Kaine."

He frowned at her words. "That's another reason I think you need to read that journal, Jennifer. Sooner or later, you're going to realize I'm not the man you think I am. We'll both be better off if you know it now, not later."

Saying nothing, Jennifer studied him carefully for a long time. Finally, she dropped her hand from his shoulder and hugged the notebook tightly against her heart. "Will you just tell me one thing, Dan? Why are you so determined that I . . . learn to accept life the way you do? Why does it matter so much to you?"

He didn't respond right away. Finally, he reached for her hand and, going to the couch, sat down with her beside him. "Jennifer, I love you too much to ignore your hurt, the pain I hear in your voice," he said quietly, still clasping her hand. "With all my heart, I want you to be able to surrender that pain to the Lord."

He drew her closer. "I just want to help you see that once you stop fighting God, at that very point you win," he said. "Jennifer, the Lord will never, ever give you less than his best. Even when life brings loss or suffering or a broken heart, God knows exactly what he's doing. He can redeem anything and turn it to good."

Jennifer studied his strong, kind face, wishing she could simply take what he seemed so determined to give, at the same time knowing it could never be that easy for her. "Daniel . . . how can I possibly accept what I don't even *understand?*"

Dan moved closer, gently coaxing her head onto his shoulder. "That's your problem, love," he said quietly, stroking her hair. "You try to *understand* first. The fact is, though, that understanding isn't the issue. There will always be things that are beyond our understanding. That's why it's absolutely vital that we take God on faith and just trust his love — for ourselves, and for others."

He seemed to choose his next words with great care. "We see today, Jennifer, but God sees eternity. We yearn for our comforts, but he wants our maturity, even if that maturity entails pain. In our search for happiness, we live for ourselves. But God says, 'Die to yourself. Live for *me.*' "

Silence hung between them for several minutes as Jennifer searched her heart for a response, only to find none. "Daniel . . . it isn't that I don't want — what you have. I *do* want it! I want it with all my heart. I've been a Christian for most of my life, but I still don't have the kind of faith you're talking about. It seems so easy for you. But it's not easy for me, Daniel! Not at all."

He went on stroking her hair. "Jennifer, whatever faith I have was a gift. God gave it to me only after I stopped ramming my head against his will."

He paused, then went on. "This may not make much sense to you, but I can tell you truthfully that I never knew the meaning of peace until after the accident — after I lost my sight."

He must have felt Jennifer tense in his arms, because he nodded and smiled. "It's true. The Lord used that time to teach me something I might never have learned otherwise. Oddly enough," he said, "I found my personal key to faith in the book of the Bible I was named after — the book of Daniel.

"Remember when King Nebuchadnezzar warned Shadrach, Meshach, and Abednego that unless they worshiped the golden image, he would toss them into the fire? I had read that story for years," he said, smiling faintly, "without ever paying much attention to their answer. But once their words really sank into my heart, I knew that I had discovered an entirely different kind of faith than I'd ever known existed. They told the king that their God 'was able to deliver' them out of the fiery furnace — but that even if he *didn't*, they weren't going to stop worshiping God and start bowing down to an idol."

Jennifer moved in his arms just enough

that she could more clearly see his face. When she did, she wondered at the expression of almost youthful enthusiasm that now lined his features. "It was like being struck by lightning," he said. "I had accepted Christ as my Savior when I was just a boy. But I had never let him be sovereign in my life — I had always stopped short of allowing him to be my Lord and Master. What I finally came to realize, after the accident, was that Christ has the right to either deliver me or *not* deliver me." He paused. "But I *don't* have the right to base my love for him and my trust in him on what he does for *me*. He's already given his life for me. *That's* what I base my faith on — the Cross. Nothing else."

Something deep within Jennifer's spirit began to stir ever so slightly. Dan's words had struck a distant chord, and now she thought she could almost catch a glimpse of a light she had thought extinguished, a hope she had lost sight of long ago.

She still didn't understand. But somehow she knew he was talking about a kind of peace that would change her life. Slowly, she lifted her head to study him. "Daniel," she said finally, "will you pray for me?"

His smile was immediate and wonderfully tender. "Love of my heart," he said in a voice rough with emotion, "I have been praying for you since that first day you crashed into my life. Why would I stop now?"

FOURTEEN

Late Wednesday afternoon, everyone at the station was racing against the clock in preparation for the radiothon on Friday. Jennifer and Dan had been swamped all day, trying to clear up last-minute details between their spots on the air, advertising meetings, and eleventh-hour instructions to other members of the staff.

They were about to finish up the afternoon drivetime. Dan had volunteered to help Jennifer jock her show so she could move in and out of the studio to work on other projects as necessary.

"I put that cart you wanted Jay to use this evening right on top," Jennifer said as the last selection came to an end. "And an extra copy of tomorrow's log so he can double-check it."

Dan nodded, waited a few seconds, then opened his mike for the last spot of the afternoon.

". . . Just a quick reminder about the weekend radiothon." He spoke into the microphone in his slow and easy drawl. "Beginning Friday night at eight o'clock, we're going to furnish you with thirty-six straight hours of your favorite Christian music, some guests you won't want to miss, and, of course, our own Jennifer Terry, doing her incomparable imitation of Mighty Minnie Mouth. . . ."

Grinning, he took a good-natured stab at Gabe, then turned serious. "On the sober side, people —" Jennifer groaned at his unintended pun — "if you turn the station on even a few minutes a day, you already know what we're doing this weekend. We're hoping for a flood of phone calls, letters, and donations to help us put some serious pressure on the people who make this country's drunk driving laws."

He paused for only an instant, long enough for his tone to turn grave. "Most of you know me, so you know that I'm a victim of a drunk driver — one victim among thousands of others. I'm blind because of someone else's lack of judgment and disregard for human life. But, friends, I'm one of the *lucky* ones."

Jennifer caught her breath, fascinated by what she was hearing. She had heard some very straight talk from Dan since he'd begun to advertise the radiothon, but not like this. The expression on his face was steady and calm, but she knew him well enough to know that he disliked any mention of his disability over the air. He was always extremely careful not to exploit his blindness. He wouldn't consider a "personal pitch," as he referred to it, unless he was convinced it would benefit someone else.

"I'm more fortunate than many others," he continued. "I survived. I'm *alive*. A lot of victims of drunk drivers don't live to protest. I did. And quite frankly, I don't like what happened to me. I had something very precious taken away, and I had absolutely nothing to say about it. But thousands of people every year — many of them not yet old enough to vote — lose their *lives*. That's what this weekend is all about. I'm asking you to stay with us for those thirty-six hours and listen to some of the things we hope to achieve with these nationwide radiothons, then do your part to help. Please."

After a moment, he closed his mike, took off his headset, and walked slowly out of the studio as if he had just completed a routine broadcast. Jennifer followed him, tears in her eyes and an enormous lump in her throat. She was so proud of him she could have wept, yet so angry at what had been done to him she would have lashed out in fury had there been somewhere to strike.

Two hours later, she was still in her office, sorting through programming schedules for the weekend, checking the log, and trying to get as many details as possible buttoned down for Gabe. She was bone-tired. She had planned on leaving before five today, but there had simply been too much to do.

Dan had promised her three days off after the radiothon, and she knew she was going to need the break. Even though she was reluctant to leave with everything that had been happening, she was still looking forward to going home.

She decided to quit for the day. She stacked the file folders on the credenza behind her desk, then left her office for Dan's.

"Dan, do you want that guest schedule tonight, or can it wait until —" She stopped just inside Dan's office when she saw Gabe and Dan with their heads together over some papers on the desk.

Gabe glanced up and gestured for her to come on in. "We're finished, Jenn."

Gabe started for the door, and Dan got to his feet. "Why don't you go on home?" he said to Jennifer. "You sound exhausted. We can finish up the rest of the schedules tomorrow."

"You don't have to coax me," Jennifer said. She turned to leave, then stopped. "You're taking Dan home?" she asked Gabe.

He nodded. "After I take him to Sager's for a chili dog."

Dan groaned and made a face, then waved Jennifer off.

In the lobby, she noticed a brown-paper package about the size of a shoe box on top of the receptionist's desk. She stopped to look, and, seeing that it was addressed to Dan, tucked it under her arm and started back down the hall.

Gabe had gone back to his office, and Dan was just putting Sunny's harness on her when Jennifer told him about the package. "Go ahead and open it for me," he said.

"Might be the new postal scale I ordered," Jennifer said, slicing through the sealing tape with a letter opener. "Nope. It's a shoe box."

Dan straightened and came back to his desk. "I didn't order any shoes. What's in it?"

Jennifer put her purse down and pulled the lid off the box. For a moment she could do nothing but stare in horror at the contents. Her sharp cry of disgust brought an answering bark from Sunny. In an instant, Dan was at her side. Jennifer struck out at the box, pushing it away.

"Jennifer? What's wrong?"

Dan caught her arm, and Jennifer turned toward him. At the same moment, Gabe came striding back into the office, stopping when he saw Jennifer's face. "What's going on?"

Jennifer motioned to the shoe box on the desk, her gaze following Gabe's as he picked up the box and looked inside.

Gabe's reaction to the three dead mice with their eyes gouged out was as vehement as Jennifer's had been. He turned to Jennifer, his face ashen.

"Is anybody going to tell me what's wrong?" Dan's harsh question broke the silence. Jennifer looked at him, then at Gabe, whose eyes blazed with a mixture of anger and revulsion. "This is sick," he choked out. "Really sick."

Dan waited only another second or two before stepping around the desk and fumbling for the shoe box. Gabe stopped him just in time, grabbing his arm. *"Don't! Don't . . . touch it!"*

Slowly, Dan pulled his hand away. "What?" he said quietly. "What's in the box?"

It was Gabe who finally told him, his voice as hard as stone. "Field mice. Dead field mice."

Dan went pale. "Field mice?" he repeated.

"Three of them," Gabe told him. He stopped, glanced at Jennifer, then added, "Their eyes . . . they have no eyes."

Jennifer reached for Dan's hand, watching him closely.

He looked stunned. His mouth went slack, then tightened. "No eyes?" he repeated softly. Then he gave a slow nod. "Three . . . blind . . . mice."

Jennifer gripped his hand even tighter. "Kind of a weird way to make a point, isn't it?" Dan said, trying to smile, not quite managing it. His voice was low and none too steady.

Gabe pulled a piece of paper from beneath the dead mice with an expression of distaste. "There's a note," he said, his voice tight and furious.

"Read it," Dan said evenly.

Gabe read it to himself first, glanced at Jennifer, then cast a worried look at Dan.

"Read it, Gabe," Dan said again.

A muscle at the side of Gabe's mouth twitched as he cleared his throat. "It says — *This is no bluff, blind man.*"

Jennifer saw Gabe's eyes cloud dangerously. She sensed that he was close to exploding. He held up the note and began to ball his hand into a fist, as though to crumple the paper.

"Gabe — no!" Jennifer cried quickly. "Don't! We have to show it to the police!"

He stopped, looking from her to the note.

"I'll call them," he said shortly, pitching the note onto the desk.

He moved toward the phone, then stopped, turning to Dan. "This is a real psycho, Dan. He isn't just out to scare you. He means to *hurt* you." Then he picked up the phone and dialed 9-1-1.

Jennifer didn't realize how tightly she had been gripping Dan's hand until he gently pried her fingers loose and tucked her hand securely inside the crook of his arm. "You all right?" he asked quietly.

She stared up at him. "I'm frightened," she said simply. "Really frightened."

He squeezed her hand reassuringly. "It'll be all right. He may just be hoping to make us drop the radiothon."

"Oh, Dan, it's more than that, I'm sure of it! But maybe we *should* postpone the radiothon, at least until —"

He gave a deep sigh. "Jennifer . . . I can't cancel it now. Think of all the time and work and money we've sunk into it. We *have* to go ahead. If I let every kook who didn't like my choice of programming dictate what I do or don't do, I'd soon be off the air for good!"

Jennifer studied him, wondering how much of his composure was genuine. "How can you *not* be afraid, Daniel? Don't you see the significance of — this?" She pushed the shoe box farther down the table.

He pulled her a little closer. "Let's not jump to any conclusions until we talk to the police, OK? Let's see what they have to say."

The police judged the threat real enough that Daniel should have round-the-clock protection. The problem was, they simply didn't have the manpower to provide it. But they promised to work out some kind of coverage, at least throughout the radiothon.

Dan rebelled at the idea, just as Jennifer and Gabe had expected him to. But in the end, the firm, commonsense demands of the police stopped his protests. It was decided that Gabe would spend the night at Dan's house with an officer stationed outside.

When one of the policemen stated that a man would also be placed outside Jennifer's house, Dan turned sharply in the direction of the officer's voice. "You think she's in danger, too?"

The young patrolman hesitated before answering, darting a quick glance at Jennifer. "I think we don't want to take any chances, Mr. Kaine. We don't know what kind of nut case we're dealing with, and someone *was* outside Miss Terry's house the other night."

Jennifer felt a cold trickle of fear snake

down her spine, but she was far too frightened for Dan to get bogged down in worry for herself.

"Gabe," she suggested, "couldn't the two of you stay at Dan's parents — just for tonight?"

"*No.*" Dan's retort was curt and sharp.

Gabe looked at him thoughtfully. "That might not be such a bad idea, Dan —"

"And it's not a good one, either," he responded shortly. "We're not bringing my folks into this. We're not going to tell them anything about it, Gabe. Forget it."

Gabe rolled his eyes at Jennifer and shrugged. "You're the boss," he said grudgingly. "OK. Why don't we get out of here so everyone can get some rest?"

It had been years since Jennifer had spent a totally sleepless night. Not since her last week in Rome, after her hopes had been crushed by the blunt pronouncement of Maestro Paulo, had she sat in a darkened room and watched the long, tedious hours of the night plod wearily toward dawn.

Tonight seemed even more endless. The presence of the unmarked patrol car gave her no comfort. She could only think of Dan.

Finally, because she knew she might go mad by morning if she didn't find something to help her pass the hours, she placed the *Daybreak* demo tape in her tape player and lay facedown on the bed to listen. At one point, she remembered the notebook Dan had given her, but she was too keyed up to read.

An hour later, she played the tape over again. It was quite simply one of the most powerful musical scores she had ever heard. It was a musical journey, a journey through the darkness of despair — as detailed by the blind man Jesus had healed; a journey through the darkness of sin — Mary Magdalene's account; and a journey through the darkness of unbelief — a Roman soldier's experience. Each of them was searching for an end to their personal darkness. And each of them found the Light of the World in God's gift of his Son, Jesus Christ.

It was beautiful. It was unique. And Jennifer knew it contained the power to change lives. No wonder Dan was so taken with it.

For one brief moment, she ached to try the songs of Mary Magdalene. She knew in her heart that her voice was right for the music. But just as quickly, she reminded herself that her voice wasn't the problem. It was her *spirit* that could no longer sing.

FIFTEEN

On Friday evening, fifteen minutes before the beginning of the radiothon, Jennifer sat in the lounge, staring vacantly outside.

It had been what Dan called a "mizzling" day. The morning had been dreary and oppressively humid, the rest of the day even gloomier. A fine drizzle of rain was now beginning to dampen the evening — and Jennifer's mood.

She would have given almost anything for a few hours of untroubled sleep and an entire day of peace and quiet, a day in which she had to do nothing but simply *think*.

Certainly, she had a few things to think about. But the one thing she really *wanted* to think about — *needed* to think about — had to be pushed onto the back burner of her mind, at least for now. How could she hope to be objective about the fact that a man had recently declared he loved her — and had asked her to marry him — when she was in the midst of a thirty-six hour physical and emotional blitz; when her daily routine consisted of Peeping Toms and pickup truck assaults; and when the man she loved was being hounded by a psychopath?

With a heavy sigh, she turned her attention

back to the moment. Her top priority for now was just to get through this weekend, though try as she might, she couldn't shake the chilling premonition that somewhere a bomb was ticking madly away — a bomb that could explode at any second.

Although she dreaded leaving Dan — especially since the incident with the dead mice in the shoe box — she felt she *had* to go home for a few days. She hadn't seen her dad or Loren for weeks, and then only for one day; their disappointment had been painfully obvious when she had left after only a few hours.

There was also no denying the fact that she needed time away from the station — time away from *Dan*. Time to think.

Glancing out the window again, Jennifer saw a patrol car park in the station's lot and a policeman approach the sidewalk leading to the front door. The police had promised that an officer would be at the station throughout the weekend. The protection should have been reassuring, but at the moment it didn't seem to help very much.

Jennifer drained the last of her coffee and rubbed the back of her neck. With a grim smile, she decided she was beginning to feel a little like a character in an old science fiction story — a man who had been imprisoned in a room with walls slowly moving inward and a tide of water gradually seeping up through the floor. The man knew he would eventually be crushed by the walls or drown in the water; his dilemma was deciding which way he preferred to die.

Dan and Sunny came into the lounge just then. Dan looked disgustingly fresh, except for his red-rimmed eyes. As always, his clothes were neatly pressed, his grooming impeccable.

Jennifer glanced down at her own outfit, a hasty, last-minute selection she'd had to settle on this afternoon when she realized that most of her clothes were in the laundry basket. Her sweater was a size too big and tended to hang in a lopsided slouch over her waist, and her slacks could have done with a good pressing.

"Jennifer?" Dan stopped a few yards from her chair.

"Be with you in a minute. As soon as I finish sticking pins in my arm to see if I'm still alive."

His smile was affectionate. "You didn't sleep either?" He was to have napped on the couch in his office while Jennifer rested at home for a few hours that afternoon. But from the looks of his eyes, he hadn't slept all that much.

"Not really. But why is it that I look like a bag lady while you look as if you've been posing for TV commercials?"

"What kind of commercials?"

"Oh, you know the ones — the guy has perfect hair and perfect teeth, and he's leaning back on a fencepost with his face lifted to the wind while he watches a gorgeous white stallion gallop through the heather on the hill."

"You didn't say anything about a perfect nose."

"You noticed, huh?"

She studied his face, unable to stop a tug of tenderness that made her heart turn over. "So — how are you, boss?" she asked him softly.

He shrugged. "OK. I rested a little."

"Good thing, since we have the first shift. Speaking of which, we'd better be getting to the studio."

Dan yawned deeply and followed her out the door. "Katharine said she put a fresh pot of coffee and cups in the studio. We must look pretty bad."

"Nah. Batman and Robin, in charge as usual. Come on, let's go wake up Shepherd Valley."

"I think we'd better wake each other up first."

★ ★ ★

Dan and Jennifer stayed on the air until eleven that night, then yielded to Gabe and Jay Regan for three hours. As they walked down the hall from the studio, Dan told Jennifer about a phone call he had received that afternoon.

The supervisor at the county children's home, Mrs. Grayson, had called to tell him that a couple had recently inquired into adopting a special child. They were interested in an older child, not an infant, and specifically wanted a boy.

They stopped at the door of Jennifer's office, and she studied him with concern. "Are they considering Jason?"

He nodded. "Mrs. Grayson said she'd like to talk to me about it before she interviews the couple. She wanted me to come in today or tomorrow, but when I explained about the radiothon, she offered to come up to the house Sunday afternoon."

Jennifer could tell that he was shaken by this unexpected news. "You're upset, aren't you?"

He bent down to release Sunny from her harness, then stood and leaned against the doorframe of Jennifer's office.

"To tell you the truth, I'm not exactly sure *how* I feel about it." He crossed his arms over his chest, saying nothing for a moment. "I just want whatever's best for Jason," he finally said. "And I've never been convinced that living with me would be the best thing for him. A single parent — who's also blind . . ." He shrugged. "I used to think that he might be just as well off at the children's home. I hadn't thought much about someone wanting to adopt him, though I suppose I should have realized it might happen."

A faint, sad smile touched his lips, then faded. "Can I ask you something? Just supposing you might agree to marry me — how would you feel about a . . . ready-made family?" As if he sensed her surprise, he quickly added, "Does Jason still make you uncomfortable?"

"I don't — it isn't that he makes me uncomfortable," Jennifer said carefully. "I just feel so *sorry* for him! Dan, we can't talk about this right now —"

"I know," he assured her quickly. "I'm not being fair to you. One crisis at a time is enough, right?" His smile was tender as he reached out to touch her hair. "Tired?"

"Mm. Not me. I'm past fatigue. I'm now into the zonk stage."

"The what?"

"Zonk. Total collapse. The mind shuts down but the mouth goes on."

"Oh. Kind of like the way Gabe is all the time."

"Exactly."

He nodded and started to turn away. "I'll have someone call you in about three hours."

"Gently, Daniel. Tell them to be sure and call me very, very gently, otherwise —" A distant rumble interrupted her in midsentence. "What was that?"

"What was *what?*"

"That noise."

"*That* noise?" he asked right after another low growl of thunder echoed far away. "I believe," he said sagely, "that's the sound of an approaching storm."

"A *thunderstorm?* At this time of year? We had snow a few days ago!"

"You're in the mountains now, love. The temperature can move up — as it has over the past few hours — or down with no warning. It's not unusual for us to have some nifty storms this time of year, once it starts to warm up."

"Oh." Jennifer shivered.

"What's wrong?"

"Nothing," she said quickly, her voice a half-tone higher than usual.

"No," he drawled softly. "I don't believe it. Not you."

"What?"

"You're afraid of storms?"

"Who said I'm afraid of storms? Did I say I'm afraid of storms?"

"You *are*, aren't you?" He brushed the knuckles of one hand lightly under her chin.

Jennifer shrugged, trying to keep her voice light. "I don't exactly *like* storms, I suppose, but I wouldn't say I'm *afraid* of them."

"I see." He grinned down at her and tapped her lightly under the chin once more. "What *would* you say?"

"Terrified," she said after a second. "I'd probably say terrified."

He shook his head in disbelief. "Well, somehow I think that once you hit that couch, you'll forget all about the storm." He tousled her hair affectionately. "Now go on — sack out while you can."

Dan's last thought before drifting off to sleep was that he might have been wrong after all. Maybe the radiothon wasn't going to bring his psycho caller out from under his rock. Maybe nothing would happen. Maybe he needn't worry about the rest of the weekend. . . .

And then he was on the mountain road again . . . but this time it was different, totally different. The nightmare propelled him at a dizzying speed past the headlights, past the crunch of metal, past his own terrified scream. He saw the flashes of color again, like last time. He knew he was dreaming, but he couldn't stop it, couldn't stop the car or the dream or even slow things down. He was slammed against the wheel, tossed back and forth against the seat, then against the wheel again. And the truck just kept right on coming, closer, closer, faster than ever before. There was a face — no, it was only an open mouth, no face — just someone screaming at him in anger . . . or in fear . . . and then he was back at the beginning. It was starting all over again, and he knew what was going to happen . . . he would feel the pain and the mind-freezing terror again. He had to stop the nightmare or it was going to kill him this time . . . the truck wasn't going to take his sight, it was going to take his life, and he had to stop it. . . .

He *couldn't* stop it; there was something he had to see, something he'd forgotten, and it was desperately important that he remember . . . now, right now. He had to go a little closer, even let himself be hurt, so this time he'd remember, this time he would know. . . .

"Dan! Daniel! Wake up! Dan!" Jennifer was shaking him gently, framing his perspiration-soaked face between her hands. "It's all right," she murmured. "You're just dreaming, Dan. It's all right, I'm here . . . it's all right now."

Dan threw an arm over his face to shield himself from the pain, to stop the truck.

"Jennifer?"

"Yes." Her voice was shaky, and he knew he must have frightened her. "Are you all right, Dan?" She wrapped her arms around him, burying her face against his shoulder. "You must have had an awful nightmare."

Dan couldn't answer her yet, couldn't quite focus his mind. Jennifer was with him, but where were they? He blinked his eyes once, then again. It was still dark. He couldn't see.

Then he remembered. And the memory hit him with the cold thud of sick reality, just as it had every morning for over five years. He couldn't see because he was blind. He wasn't ever going to see again.

He let Jennifer hold him, secretly drawing what calm he could from her, allowing himself to be soothed by her. He was always alone after the nightmare. There was never anyone to comfort him, to ease the terror. With grateful relief, he let Jennifer hold him now and murmur softly to him until he could face the darkness again.

SIXTEEN

By Saturday night Dan knew what he had to do. Even though there hadn't been so much as a minor incident during the radiothon, which would end tomorrow morning, all his instincts told him something was going to happen and that this weekend would somehow trigger whatever it was.

He had decided to go on the offensive. If at all possible, he wanted to put an end to this madness while Jennifer was safely out of harm's way. She would leave by noon tomorrow to visit her family in Athens. That meant he had two days to take the initiative, to provoke his tormentor to make a move.

He thought he knew how to go about it. But he would have to wait. First, he intended to make certain that Jennifer was gone.

The man in the pickup truck sat staring at the back of the radio station, his view distorted by the rain slashing the windshield. Occasionally, his eyes would flick back and forth in rhythm with the halting, noisy scrape of the windshield wipers. Mostly he stared straight ahead.

Anticipation quickened his breathing. He rolled down the window a few inches and tossed a half-smoked cigarette outside onto the saturated ground, immediately pulling another from the pack in his jacket pocket. Squeezing it tightly between his nicotine-stained fingers, he squinted as the smoke from the match burned his eyes.

It was late, but the radio station was only dimly lighted. No more than half a dozen cars were in the parking lot, including the black Cherokee that belonged to the station, the Terry woman's Honda, and Denton's Thunderbird. And a police cruiser.

He curled his lip as he stared at the patrol car. He hadn't counted on the police staying this late. He had waited all evening, his pick-up safely hidden behind the brush and pine trees on the hill. But the cruiser was still there.

His chest tightened painfully, and the sour taste in his mouth grew even more rancid. He might just as well go home for the night.

He fiddled with the radio dial. Even this close, the station was laced with static, the night sparked with electricity. A gospel song came over the air, and he turned it off with a snap.

Kaine hadn't been on the air for a long time. He wondered what he was doing in there. Not that it mattered. He wasn't going to be able to finish him tonight anyway. He'd have to wait till tomorrow. But that was all right. Kaine would be worn out by then. And he wouldn't be surrounded by so many people. Maybe it would be even better, easier to take care of him at home. Alone.

By seven Sunday morning, Dan knew he could delay no longer. The radiothon would end in an hour. Jennifer was down the hall, briefing Jay Regan and Gabe, who would be handling the regular Sunday broadcasting; she wouldn't hear him on the air. He opened his mike, took a deep, steadying breath, and began to speak. "And now a word for my friend in the noisy pickup truck." He paused, then went on. "I got your package. And your messages. Now I've got a message for *you*." He kept his voice level as he spoke softly into the mike.

"I know who you are. And I know what you're doing, and why. So let's stop playing games. I've known what you want for a long time now. And after this weekend is over, the police will know everything *I* know." He hesitated for an instant, then added, *"The blind man is calling your bluff, pal."*

He turned off his mike, quickly cued up another song, and said a brief, silent prayer.

You and I both know it's me who's bluffing, Lord. I don't have a clue who this nut is, but I've got to make him show himself while Jen-

nifer's gone. I have this sick feeling that he might try to get at me through her. I don't know what else to do, Lord. I can't shake the thought that I'm running out of time, that he's closing in. I have to force his hand now, before someone besides me gets hurt. . . .

The man hurled his coffee cup across the room, his eyes blazing as the pieces shattered on the wall and fell to the floor.

Big-mouthed ape! Who did he think he was, anyway? Talking to the whole town like that!

His eyes were watering, and he wiped them on a dirty sleeve, then slumped down onto the torn plastic seat of a kitchen chair. So, he'd been right all along. Kaine *did* know. But he must not have known too long. Otherwise, he would have done something about it before now.

Well, it was a good thing he'd already planned to get rid of him. Once Kaine blabbed to the police, it would be too late.

They'd never believe me, not against that blind self-righteous hypocrite! The whole town thinks he's some kind of a saint or something. Who's going to take my word against his?

Well, after today he wouldn't have to worry anymore. With Kaine out of the picture, no one would ever know the truth. He'd be safe. Finally safe.

SEVENTEEN

Dan missed her already, and it was only one o'clock. Jennifer hadn't even been gone three hours yet, but her absence was like a hole in his heart.

If it hurt this much when she left him for two days, how would he live with it if she refused to marry him, if he had to settle for living on the outside fringes of her life forever? She was as important to him as breathing by now. Without her, he'd just be taking up space.

Oh, Lord, you know how much I love her. I've let myself believe that you brought her into my life for me to love, to marry. But what if I'm wrong? What if I'm wrong?

Would she talk to her father and brother about him? Would they try to discourage her from getting involved with a blind man? With a stab of apprehension, he realized he couldn't blame them if they did. If Jennifer were his daughter, he might do the same. How many fathers would encourage their daughters to marry a person with his disability?

He sank down onto the piano bench, letting his fingers run idly over the keys with no purpose other than to fill the emptiness of his house with sound . . . any sound. It seemed strange to be alone. Of course, it wouldn't last. But he was glad for it now, at least.

He had tried to put Gabe's mind at rest about leaving him alone for the afternoon, insisting it was more important that Gabe be at the station the rest of the day. Gabe had agreed only after Dan promised to have Lyss or his dad pick him up as soon as his appointment with Mrs. Grayson was finished.

Dan had already called the police and told them they needn't keep an eye on the house this afternoon, that he'd be leaving shortly. Now he had nothing to do but wait for Mrs. Grayson. He had every intention of leaving the house as soon as she did.

Earlier he had almost decided to spend the afternoon alone, waiting for his psychotic friend to make a move. But he had finally admitted to himself that he wasn't that brave. Or that stupid.

He was beginning to think his scheme to lure his unknown adversary into the open had been full of holes from the beginning. Because he'd been so determined to force his assailant's hand during Jennifer's absence, he had ignored the fact that, if this nut came after him while he was alone, there was very little he could do to stop him. Even Sunny would be little help in a situation like that.

Besides, while his first thought had been to protect Jennifer, he didn't want anyone *else* getting hurt either.

Preoccupied by his thoughts when the doorbell rang, he misstepped on his way to answer it and stubbed his toe against the rolltop desk. He opened the door, appalled to discover that Jason was with Mrs. Grayson.

"I hope you don't mind my bringing him along, Dan," the superintendent said as they entered. "But he's missed you terribly the last few days, and I thought it might be good for the two of you to spend a few minutes together."

Dan hesitated, then replied, "Sure. That's fine. Jason, you can play with Sunny while I talk with Mrs. Grayson."

In truth, he was disturbed that Jason had come. He was tense and edgy enough without having to worry about something happening to the boy. But he managed a smile and a playful cuff on the chin before sending him off with Sunny to the loft.

"I'm sorry I haven't been able to spend any time with him this week," Dan said as they sat down in the living room. "I explained about the radiothon —"

"I understand," Mrs. Grayson assured him. "But the child has become terribly attached to you, Daniel, and he's unhappy when he's away from you for any length of time. That's what I wanted to talk about."

Dan remained silent while she told him about the inquiry she had received from the prospective adoptive couple. "I just wanted to be completely sure you weren't interested in adopting Jason yourself before going any further."

Surprised, Dan hesitated for a moment before answering. "I *would* be interested — very interested — if I weren't blind . . . and single."

"I understand that. But I've seen you and the boy together, Daniel, and quite frankly I have my doubts that a physically perfect couple can meet Jason's needs any better than you can — if as well."

Caught off guard by her words, Dan was uncertain how to reply. "There would be problems," he began.

"There are *always* problems when you become a parent," she said, and Dan could hear the smile in her voice. "But I've worked with children and adoptive parents for years, and I've seen some otherwise insurmountable problems overcome by plenty of love and common sense."

"I *do* love the boy," Dan said thoughtfully. "And I'd jump at the chance to have him with me if I thought I wouldn't be cheating him."

"How could *loving* the boy possibly be *cheating* him?" Mrs. Grayson gave Dan no time to respond. "If you should decide to pursue the idea, it might be advisable for you to fill out a preliminary application. It wouldn't bind you to anything," she assured him quickly. "But it would let us get started on a home study and reference check. And it would allow me to place you in the file for consideration as a prospective parent. In addition to others, of course."

Dan rubbed one hand over his chin, then gave a small nod of his head and smiled. "There's someone I'd like to discuss this with, Mrs. Grayson. Would I be hurting my chances if I waited until the middle of the week to turn in an application?"

After encouraging Dan to take his time and consider his decision carefully, Mrs. Grayson rose to leave.

They called Jason and Sunny downstairs, but the boy begged Dan to let him stay. "Just while Mrs. Grayson does her errands, Dan. Please? I'll be real quiet."

Dan was uncomfortable about being alone at the house with Jason right now, but he couldn't explain that to the boy. Finally, he agreed that Jason could stay, but only until Mrs. Grayson returned from her errands.

Jason and Sunny trooped off to play in the yard while Dan walked Mrs. Grayson to her car. The superintendent advised him not to say anything to Jason that would give him false hope, but did suggest that the two of them might at least discuss the possibility of adoption.

After her car pulled away, Dan called Jason to him. "Let's give Sunny a few minutes to run, now that the rain has stopped," he told the boy. "She's been cooped up inside the station with me all weekend."

The afternoon was heavy with a thick humidity. Dan let Sunny romp off, knowing she'd return to check on them now and then. Besides, Jason liked the idea of guiding Dan around the yard, and they usually made a game of it.

"There's something I'd like to talk about, sport," Dan said, taking Jason by the hand.

"What, Dan?" The boy's tone was distracted. Obviously, his attention was more on Sunny than the conversation.

Dan proceeded to tell the child, simply and sincerely, how he felt about him. "You're very special to me, Jason. I like being with you, and I love you very much.

In fact, you're like my own little boy. That's how much I care about you. Do you understand that?"

They stopped walking, and Dan felt Jason clasp his hand even tighter. "I love you, too, Dan," the boy said. He surprised Dan with his immediate, sober response and his perception. "And I wish you were my daddy."

Dan felt a little tug at his heart when he heard how small and serious Jason sounded. "Why, Jason?" he prompted. "Why would you want me to be your daddy?"

"So I could stay with you forever."

After a pause, Dan asked, "You'd like that, would you? To stay with me, even though you might never have a mother?"

Jason considered that for a moment. "I'd like to have a mother, too. But I wouldn't be sad without one if you were my daddy." Then something else occurred to him. "Maybe Jennifer would like to be my mother. I think she likes me. And I *know* she likes you!"

Dan's grin was a quick flash of pleasure at Jason's words. "You think so, huh?" Laughing, he picked the boy up and swung him to his shoulder, then set him lightly to his feet.

The retriever bounded over at the sound

of laughter, eager to be included. Suddenly she stopped, alert to a sound the others had missed.

Her instinct, born of long, intensive training, years of experience — and immeasurable love — was to immediately ignore her own desire to play, even to ignore the fact that she wasn't on her harness. Moving like a fireball, she hurled herself directly at her master.

The dog took the first bullet in her side and yelped. The boy, thinking the retriever wanted to play, jumped toward her. He caught the second bullet.

Dan heard Sunny's shriek of pain, then heard Jason go down with a surprised cry. In one lightning-fast instant, he realized what he had heard — and knew the shots had missed their intended target.

With the third explosion, he reacted by raw instinct, pitching to the ground in an attempt to remove himself as a target. After another second or two, he choked out Jason's name, then called for Sunny.

No sound broke the deadly quiet on the mountain. He could hear nothing but the pounding of his heart as he lay, silently waiting. He forced himself to lie perfectly still, hoping the sniper would think he'd been hit.

He'll eventually come to make sure he got me.

The thought froze him with panic. He felt his skin grow cold and wet with perspiration, and he thought he might be sick. He swallowed hard against the hot taste of bile rising in his throat. He wanted desperately to reach out and grope for Sunny or Jason, but he didn't dare.

He was totally helpless, a sitting duck. There was nothing he could do, no way he could help Jason and Sunny.

He didn't even know for certain where they were. They might still be alive, but they would bleed to death if he didn't get help for them.

Help me . . . merciful God, help me. . . .

He stiffened, held his breath, and suddenly his entire body began to tremble. He heard an engine, someone coming up the driveway. He clenched his teeth together until the tension hurt his jaw, forcing himself not to move, not to cry out. Was it a truck? He tensed even more, then melted with relief. No. Closer now, he knew it was a car. It couldn't be Mrs. Grayson coming back; it was too soon. But the car was familiar.

His dad's Lincoln! *Thank you . . . oh, my dear Lord, thank you. . . .*

Then he realized he had to warn his dad. He couldn't let his father pull in the driveway and get out of the car without knowing

— he had to warn him.

He waited until the solid, powerful sound of the big engine slowed as it turned into the driveway, waited until the exact instant the ignition died before pushing himself to his knees and hauling himself upright to wave his hands and shout a warning.

EIGHTEEN

The steady downpour of rain had been with her since she left Athens, turning the road outside her windshield into an eerie, distorted rivulet. But Jennifer had cried so hard since her frantic departure that she no longer knew whether it was her tears or the rainstorm obscuring the road.

Lyss's call that evening had come only hours after Jennifer's arrival at home. She had been so badly shaken by the news that her dad begged her to stay overnight and leave in the morning. But she couldn't possibly have waited, had instead thrown her things back into her suitcase and, kissing her father and Loren good-bye, had started for West Virginia.

The ache at the back of her neck was nothing compared to the ache in her heart as she remembered her conversation with Lyss. "Dan told me not to call you, Jennifer, but Gabe said I should."

Lyss's voice had been frightened and strained as she relayed the bad news about Jason and Sunny. She had gone on to explain that, according to the police, the shots had been fired from a high-powered hunting rifle, probably from the upper side of the hill behind Dan's house. The sniper's getaway would have been easy and quick.

Jason had still been unconscious when Lyss called Jennifer. Fortunately, the shot had just grazed him — but the boy must have hit his head on a rock when he fell, causing a concussion. Lyss's father had indicated it might be several hours before they had a clearer picture of the child's condition.

As for Sunny, apparently she had been hit in the side. The vet seemed to think she would be all right, but it was too soon to be sure.

Jennifer couldn't bear to think what this had done to Daniel, although Lyss had been painfully honest about her concern for her brother.

"Physically, Dan is fine," she had assured Jennifer. But as she'd gone on, Jennifer had realized that she was weeping quietly, even as they spoke. "He's so . . . *shattered,* Jennifer! And he's blaming himself for the whole thing!"

Lyss explained then how Dan had deliberately tried to bait his tormentor into making a move while Jennifer was gone.

Dismayed that he would have endangered himself on her behalf, Jennifer remained silent while Lyss continued.

"You're not going to find the same Dan you

left, Jennifer," she had warned. "I haven't seen him this way since the accident."

Now Jennifer wiped at her eyes, squinting against the monotonous swipe of the windshield wipers. Lyss's final words evoked the memory of what her father had said upon learning of her love for Dan — and his proposal — before they'd heard about the shootings.

"You know, Jenny —" no one but her father ever called her Jenny — "I think the secret of your Daniel's remarkable spirit is that he's placed it in the hands of a loving God, a God who is far, far wiser than any of us. Daniel has allowed God to work his will in whatever way he chooses, even through a tragedy like blindness."

Steven Terry's dark brown eyes had studied Jennifer for a long time. "That's how it was with your mother, too. Even in those last few days at the hospital, just before she died, she allowed the Lord to use her illness — to use *her* — to make a difference for others."

His eyes had misted and his voice had been unsteady as he explained. "You need to know, Jenny, that there are at least half a dozen lives somewhere out there that might never have been changed if it hadn't been for your mother's faith." He had paused a moment before going on. "I believe with all my heart that, if she could, your mother would tell you to look for the glory in things, not the grief."

Jennifer was trying, but at the moment she was finding it almost impossible to see any glory.

Well after eleven, she drove into town, the rain coming down so hard she could just barely make out the red lights of the radio tower on the hill. For some inexplicable reason, the sight of the tower saddened her. Dan's life revolved around that station — he ate, lived, and breathed it. It was that way with Jason and Sunny, too — they had become such an essential part of Dan's life.

She felt a wrench of dismay as she realized that it almost seemed as though Dan were being cut off from everything that mattered most to him.

The thought made her press the gas pedal a little harder. Suddenly it seemed absolutely vital that she get to Dan as quickly as possible.

She found him at the hospital with Lyss and Gabe. She stopped short for a moment when she got off the elevator on the second floor. She could see the three of them sitting in the small lounge at the far end of the hall.

Taking a deep breath to steady herself, she began walking down the corridor toward them.

Gabe stood as soon as he saw her and gave her a weak smile. Lyss also got to her feet, glancing from Jennifer to Dan, who sat woodenly, his head buried in both hands.

He raised his head when he heard her approaching steps. Jennifer thought uneasily that his features registered no real surprise or pleasure, only a kind of sullenness.

"Jennifer?" His tone was as wooden as his expression.

Now that she was close enough to get a good look at him, Jennifer felt almost ill with dismay. She found it difficult to respond to Lyss's welcoming hug or Gabe's quick squeeze of her hand. Instead, she could only stare with concern at Dan. His hair needed combing, his blue sweatshirt was spotted with what appeared to be grass stains and blood, and his face was haggard, engraved with stark, grim lines of fatigue and worry. Other than voicing her name, he made no move to acknowledge her presence.

She took a deep breath, then forced herself to stoop down beside him. "Dan — are you all right?" She covered his hands with her own, but he held himself rigid, unmoving, offering only a small nod to her question.

"Jason — how is he?"

When Dan didn't answer, Jennifer looked up at Gabe and then Lyss, who shook her head. "No change. He's still unconscious."

Returning her attention to Dan, Jennifer studied him, still hoping for some sign of welcome. Finally he spoke. "Who called you?"

"Lyss. She knew I'd want to be here."

"She told you what happened then," he said heavily.

"Yes. Oh, Dan . . . I'm so sorry. I know how much they both mean to you." She paused, then tried to reassure him. "They're going to be all right, Dan."

He slumped back against the chair. "Even now," he said thickly, "we still don't know who he is."

"But we'll find out," Jennifer insisted, getting to her feet. She turned to Gabe. "Haven't the police learned anything yet?"

With a look of abject frustration, Gabe shook his head. "Not a clue."

Just then Lucas Kaine, a big, silver-haired model of his son, walked out of a room a few doors down and approached them. Jennifer thought Lucas appeared to be as exhausted as Dan. But his eyes lighted when he saw her standing there, and he managed a smile for her.

"Jennifer, I'm so glad you're here." He darted a quick glance at his son. "There's no change, Dan. I just checked Jason again."

His gaze took in everyone at once. "I think all of you should go home now and get some rest." He held up a restraining hand when Lyss started to object. "Jason will be monitored throughout the night. That's all we can do right now." He hesitated, then added sternly, "You look terrible — every one of you. You're not doing anyone any good this way."

He then turned a meaningful look on Gabe. "I want Dan to stay with us tonight. Will you take him out to the house? I'm going to stick around here for another hour or so."

Gabe hesitated and looked uneasily at Dan, who simply gave a brief shake of his head. "I'm staying with Jason. In case he wakes up."

With an uncertain glance at Lucas, Gabe closed the distance between himself and Dan. "Dan, you're not going to accomplish anything except to wear yourself out," he told his friend.

"I'm staying," Dan said flatly.

With a tired sigh, Lucas met Gabe's eyes and shrugged. "All right. If that's what you want, son."

"Take me to the room, please, Gabe," Dan said dully.

Gabe looked at Dan with surprise, as if he'd just become aware of Sunny's absence. He reached out tentatively to take Dan's arm. "Sure, buddy. This way."

Surprised and disturbed, Jennifer watched as Dan docilely allowed Gabe to lead him down the hall to Jason's room. He hadn't even told her goodnight. She had to fight back tears of pain and rejection as she watched the two of them walk away. Dan's shoulders were slumped, his steps uncertain and shuffling.

For the first time since she'd met him, Jennifer thought with sick despair, Dan actually looked . . . blind.

NINETEEN

Over the next few days Jennifer saw all too clearly what Lyss had meant about Dan not being the same.

On the surface, he seemed to go about his usual routine. He went to work. He went home — although "home" had temporarily become his parents' house. He went to visit Jason at the hospital and Sunny at the vet's. Although Jason remained unresponsive, the doctors were still hopeful that his condition would improve. As for Sunny, she seemed to be recovering nicely. She recognized her visitors and nuzzled Dan's hand lovingly when he approached.

Somehow, it was Dan who seemed to be the most wounded of the three. He had become an empty reflection of his former self. His sustaining sense of humor, his upbeat disposition — even his warmth — had all but vanished. He came to the station but stayed out of the studio, remaining in his office to work behind closed doors. He ate most of his meals alone at his desk, and Jennifer knew that much of his food ended up in the trash can. If he happened to venture into the lounge when others were present, he sat quietly drinking his coffee, never really participating in the conversation. Even to Jennifer, he was merely courteous, but impersonal and distant.

He had taken to walking with a cane and wearing dark glasses, both of which had come as a shock to Jennifer. The first time she saw him with the unfamiliar gear she wanted to weep for him and, at the same time, shake him.

As if he had sensed her surprise — and possibly her disappointment — he made a lame effort to explain. "Without Sunny, I'm a bit of a menace," he said. "I stumble easily, bump into things. The cane helps me to avoid breaking my neck. That and the dark glasses let others know I'm blind."

When Jennifer offered the cautious observation that Sunny's absence was only temporary — a few days at the most — he said nothing, but merely went on down the hall, the cane tapping in front of him on the way.

Gabe hated the cane and the glasses as much as Jennifer did. "When Dan came back from Seeing Eye with Sunny," he told her, "he said he'd *never* use that 'despicable cane' again. Those were his exact words." He went on to explain that, although the cane and dark glasses were perfectly acceptable props, it bothered him that Dan had come to rely on them again. "I can't help but think it's just another indication of how depressed he really is."

Jennifer made every effort to return their relationship to what it had been, all to no avail. Her attempts at humor bombed hopelessly; her not-so-subtle hints that he was avoiding her seemed to fall on deaf ears. Dan had shut her out, along with everyone else. And there seemed to be nothing she could do about it.

By Wednesday evening, she was physically and emotionally exhausted. Combined with Dan's bewildering and painful rejection was her continual concern for Jason and Sunny — not to mention the grim reality that somewhere out there a lunatic was still loose, and more than likely still bent on hurting Dan.

At the moment, she could think of nothing else but Dan. She had left the station earlier than usual, bogged down in a black mood that was growing worse by the minute. Driven by sheer desperation to find something — anything — that would help her understand what Dan was going through, she now sat at her kitchen table, hunched intently over his journal. She didn't know what she was looking for — perhaps some kind of magic key that would unlock the secrets of his heart so she could help him to get through this awful time.

Before tonight, she had scanned a few pages of the journal but had been reluctant to plumb the depths of emotion and insight she suspected the pages might contain. This evening, however, she began on page one, stopping only when her attention was captured, a few pages later, by something in Dan's notes, an observation that reminded her of one of the musical selections from *Daybreak*.

At the same time, a splash of color tucked in the back lining of the notebook caught her eye, and she pulled out what appeared to be a book jacket. She studied it curiously for a moment, then drew in a sharp breath of astonishment. What she held in her hands was the cover to the published musical score of *Daybreak*. It clearly identified Daniel Kaine as the composer of both lyrics and music.

Jennifer stared at the cover for several minutes, her gaze locked on Dan's name. Finally, she reached behind her to the portable tape player on the counter. The demo for *Daybreak* was still in place, and she pushed the play button to start it. Then she returned to the journal.

For the next few hours, she was held captive by this extraordinarily personal, penetrating glimpse of the mind and heart of a

man she was only now beginning to understand. It was an intensely painful process.
Her eyes often blurred by tears, Jennifer followed the spiritual and emotional journey of
a man groping his way toward the reality of
a loving God, a man seeking sanity in the
midst of a nightmare, hope in the midst of
despair, and faith in the midst of destruction.
Long after the last light of evening had
turned to darkness, she continued to trace
Dan's steps, to walk with him through the
long and dreary midnight of his soul.

She even found herself praying with him
— not the quick, routine type of prayer her
devotions had degenerated to over the past
few years, but the plea of an injured child
in the first throes of recognizing her own
need for healing.

She was there with him, beside his hospital
bed years before, when his horror-stricken
brain refused to acknowledge reality but
continued to anesthetize itself to time and
place. *In dark places he has made me dwell,*
she read, *like those who have long been
dead. . . .*

She sat by the bed and watched him fight
his way through the maze of pain and shock
and denial, felt his sickening awareness of
being violated, mutilated, and humiliated. *I
am the man who has seen affliction. He has*

driven me and made me walk in darkness and not in light. He has besieged and encompassed me with bitterness and hardship. . . .

She smelled his fear and tasted his tears, shared his anger and suffered his defeat, until she thought she could no longer bear the haunted labyrinth of his heart. *He has made me desolate . . . my soul has been rejected from peace; I have forgotten happiness. My strength has perished, and so has my hope from the Lord . . .*

But she couldn't leave him. By now she was his partner in agony as she saw him fumble his way past utter despair and finally get to his knees, then stand and begin to fight. *I have called you by name; you are mine! When you pass through the waters, I will be with you; and through the rivers, they will not overflow you. When you walk through the fire, you will not be scorched, nor will the flame burn you. . . .*

She echoed his anguished questions during those first weeks after he left the hospital, as he suffered the frustration and humiliation of dependency. *Oh, that I knew where I might find him. . . . I would present my case before him and fill my mouth with arguments. It is God who has made my heart faint, and the Almighty who has dismayed me, but I am not silenced by the darkness, nor the deep gloom which covers me. . . .*

Then, slowly and reluctantly, she began to listen with him throughout the weary days and weeks and months of searching, as God spoke and challenged and thundered his truth from the pages of his Word. *I am the Lord, and there is no other, the one forming light and creating darkness . . . I am the Lord who does all these. Who has given to me that I should repay him? Whatever is under the whole heaven is mine. . . .*

Weakly, she knelt with him in the garden of his final battle, waiting and watching as he finally admitted his humanness, his weakness, and his sin. *Who are you, O man, who answers back to God? The thing molded will not say to the molder, "Why did you make me like this," will it? Or does not the potter have a right over the clay? Behold, like the clay in the potter's hand, so are you in my hand. Woe to the one who quarrels with his maker. . . .*

She fell facedown with him in the dust and ashes of his pride as his broken, shattered spirit once and for all acknowledged the truth of his Creator, the sovereignty of his Savior, and the infinite love of his Redeemer. *My spirit is broken. I have declared that which I did not understand, things too wonderful for me, which I did not know. Shall we accept good from God and not accept adver-*

sity? I know that my Redeemer lives. . . .
Though he slay me, I will hope in him. . . .

And finally, Jennifer realized, as Daniel had, that he had been weak until the Lord made him strong . . . that he had been frightened until the Lord made him brave . . . that he had been rebellious and angry until the Lord made him gentle and kind . . . that he was no more than what his Lord had made him, and the best of what he now was had come out of the fire of affliction.

On these pages born of his pain, she saw his pride, his stubbornness, his rebellion, his fury, his fear, his denial, his doubt, and his weakness. She watched him come to the end of his own resources, humble himself, and acknowledge the majesty and sovereignty of his God. She witnessed a man broken by grief and pain transformed into a restored, whole man of God. *And the Lord blessed the latter days of Job more than his beginning . . . the Lord gave and the Lord has taken away. Blessed be the name of the Lord.*

And then Jennifer knelt and allowed the Lord to begin the same healing and renewing process in her own life, knowing this was what Daniel had meant. This was what he had wanted for her.

She wept and prayed for what seemed like hours, giving God her anger and rebellion,

her confusion and resentment and hopelessness. She gave God her fractured ego, her
shattered dreams, her broken heart.

And finally, she knew her healing had begun.

While still on her knees, Jennifer caught a
new, incisive glimpse of truth about the man
she loved more than life, a truth Dan himself
had already tried to convey to her. He was
no giant, no spiritual colossus. He was only
a man, human and imperfect and subject to
the same faults and frailties as she was. He
was a wounded hero who had fought on the
battleground of his faith — and overcome.
Through his loss, he had won; in his weakness, he had become strong; and in his surrender, he had been made much more than
a conqueror.

Jennifer had long wondered at the secret
of Dan's peace. Now, ever so slowly, that
secret began to come to light in the shadows
of her mind. Daniel had realized — and acknowledged — God's absolute right to do
with his creation as he willed. And then he
had learned to trust the Lord's love enough
to surrender his own broken heart and his
searching soul to that love. In the abyss of
his pain, he had finally thrown himself upon
the mercy of his God . . . and God had taken
the bitter dust of blindness and breathed a

new life of faith into being. This was the light that glowed from Daniel Kaine, the light at which others warmed their hearts.

But now his light was flickering and threatening to go out. He was giving in to defeat and guilt and despair. Jennifer sensed in him a weariness, a hopelessness that simply refused to fight another battle. And she understood, even sympathized with, his inclination to retreat. Once more the humiliation and despair of dependency had been thrust upon him. Added to that was his loss of pride and sense of helplessness at being unable to protect those he loved.

Jennifer ached for him. But she couldn't allow him the crutch of guilt or the comfort of self-pity. Somehow she must make him remember what he had tried so desperately to teach *her.*

In her heart, she knew she might well be the only one who could give him the will to stand and fight again.

TWENTY

By Friday evening, Jennifer knew it was time to confront Dan.

It was another odd, unseasonably warm night. The atmosphere was almost oppressive with electricity. Thunder drummed faintly in the distance, and thick, ink-black clouds hung ominously above the valley. Jennifer gripped the steering wheel, shuddering when the sky suddenly blazed with lightning.

She saw with relief that Dan's house was bathed with light, inside and out. The security light by the garage was on, as were the carriage lights on either side of the front door. Inside, the lower level was aglow throughout. The apprehension she had felt upon learning from Dan's mother that he'd returned to his house for the weekend faded when she saw a police cruiser parked on one side of the driveway.

Shepherd Valley was small enough that the police force always seemed to be short of manpower. But ever since the shooting incident with Jason and Sunny, the department had made certain that a patrolman was nearby whenever Dan had to be alone for any length of time.

According to Dan's mother, he had been

extremely restless and depressed all evening. Finally, he had insisted on going home, and Gabe had driven him.

Pauline Kaine had sounded worried. "Gabe is going back to stay the night at Dan's, but first he and Lyss are dropping by to check on Jason. I wish Dan had gone with them."

Jennifer cut the engine and got out of the car. She tucked Dan's journal under her arm, then covered it with her raincoat before hurrying up the driveway to the porch.

Rick Hill, the same patrolman who had been at her house the night of the Peeping Tom incident, unlocked the door, leaving the security chain on until he saw Jennifer. He was in uniform, and Jennifer noted uneasily that his hand was touching his holstered service revolver when he opened the door for her to enter.

"Good to see you, Miss Terry," he said politely. "Mrs. Kaine called to tell me you were coming."

Jennifer tossed her yellow slicker over a dining-room chair, holding on to the journal.

"Dan's in there," the policeman said, gesturing toward the door that led from the kitchen into the pool area. "Sounds like it's cooking up a storm outside."

Jennifer nodded. "Something's headed

this way, I'm afraid."

She pushed up the sleeves on her sweater and started toward the pool area, opening the door slowly and quietly. She stopped just inside. Dan was in the water; obviously, he hadn't heard her enter. Jennifer stood watching him with fascination, remembering Dr. Rodaven's words when he had first told her about Dan's blindness: "Kaine was a real powerhouse in the water."

He still is, Jennifer thought. But she sensed that the power now emanating from him as he thudded through the water in a perfectly executed front crawl was at least partly born of anger and frustration.

She expelled a sharp breath of appreciation as Dan reached the far end of the pool, did a lightning-fast flip turn, then roared through the water again. He was approaching her now, and she could see the mixture of anguish and rage contorting his features.

As he turned and did another lap, Jennifer glanced from the man in the water to the two photos on the pool wall — photos which, according to Dan, his mother had insisted on hanging. They had been taken at the Olympics the year he won the gold medal for the United States. A younger, beardless Dan was standing in the middle of a beaming huddle consisting of his parents,

Gabe, and Lyss. He looked pleased and flushed with victory.

Jennifer's eyes misted as she turned her gaze back to the pool. Dan had stopped in the middle of a stroke and was treading water. The strong emotions that had been playing on his features only a moment before had relaxed to a look of weary resignation.

"Dan —" Jennifer walked around to the side of the pool and stopped, waiting.

He jerked with surprise, bobbing up and down in the water a few times before making his way to the side of the pool. "Jennifer?" He hauled himself up out of the water and sat down on the edge of the pool, fumbling for a white terry cloth robe lying nearby. Jennifer stooped to hand it to him.

"Do you see my towel anywhere?" he asked, shrugging into his robe.

Saying nothing, Jennifer retrieved the towel off a nearby aluminum chair and pressed it into his hands.

"What are you doing here?" Dan's guarded tone stopped just short of being rude.

"I — thought perhaps we could talk."

His eyes narrowed as he began to towel-dry his hair. "Something wrong?"

"No," Jennifer said quickly, hesitating before going on. "But . . . I thought it was time I gave you an answer." At his puzzled expression, she added, "To your proposal."

He froze, his arms suspended above his head. An expression very much like anger settled over his features, but he remained stonily silent.

Jennifer cleared her throat and continued. "You asked me," she said as evenly as possible, "to marry you. Remember?" She held her breath, watching him.

Dan's face darkened, and for a moment he looked uncertain. Then, unbelievably, he began to dry his hair again with slow, steady motions.

"Go home, Jennifer," he said quietly but not unkindly. "Don't do this. Not now."

"Don't do what?" Jennifer clenched her hands at her sides. "Don't you want my answer?"

"Just . . . don't." His voice was hard with warning. But Jennifer instinctively understood his reaction. He thought she had come out of pity.

She had to remind herself that this was Dan. Not as she had learned to know him and not as she had grown to love him . . . but Dan, nevertheless.

"I see," she said quietly. "You weren't serious, then . . . when you asked me to marry you? When you told me you loved me?"

She knew she had hit a nerve. He actually flinched and stopped that inane, monotonous toweling of his hair. "Things are different now. I don't have to tell you that." He dropped the towel onto the chair beside him, letting his hands dangle loosely at his sides.

It struck Jennifer suddenly that he had lost weight. And she was certain there were lines fanning out from his eyes that hadn't been there a few days ago. Suppressing the pity that threatened to unnerve her, she went on. "What exactly has changed, Dan? Your feelings about me?"

He turned away from her, but before he did, Jennifer saw his face glaze with pain. "Listen," he bit out, "You don't owe me an answer. You don't owe me anything. Just go home. Please."

"No."

He pivoted around in surprise.

Please, Lord, let me get through to him. Let me reach him, help him . . . please. . . .

"Daniel, you said you loved me. Has that changed so quickly?"

"What are you *doing* here?" His voice sounded strangled.

"Humiliating myself, apparently," Jennifer replied in a small voice, determined not to cry.

"Jennifer — don't . . ."

"I came to tell you that my answer is *yes*, Daniel. I want to marry you." She could hear her own weakness in her tremulous words. "Unless, of course, you *have* changed your mind. About us."

She felt a quick stab of hope when she saw a parade of conflicting emotions begin to march across his face. But abruptly he shook his head, lifting a restraining hand as though to stop her from going any further.

"Jennifer, don't do this to me, don't —"

"And if you're thinking," Jennifer pressed on, determined to hold what small edge of advantage she had gained, "that this has anything to do with my feeling sorry for you, forget it." She deliberately sharpened her tone.

He started to reply, but she moved in even harder. "I don't feel sorry for you at all," she said firmly. "In fact, Daniel, if you want the truth, I think I'm angry with you."

His dark brows knit together in a confused frown. "What —"

"I read your journal," she said matter-of-factly. "And I have to tell you that it seems to me you've forgotten a few things."

"Now, *listen* —"

He was angry. Good. At least he was feeling *something*.

Jennifer slammed the journal down on the aluminum table near the pool. "What you wrote on those pages, Daniel," she said carefully, knowing she was treading on shaky ground, "and the glorious piece of music that came out of it, is life-changing." She paused. "I know it's changed *my* life."

The angry set of his mouth relaxed only slightly. "What are you talking about?"

"I can't help wondering, though, about some of the things you wrote in your journal. If they were true five years ago, aren't they true today?" She took a deep breath, then decided that after going this far, she couldn't quit now. "Has God changed in the meantime?"

She was amazed at her own insolence. She prayed she wasn't going beyond the point of forgiveness.

"What exactly are you getting at?" The anger he was so obviously fighting to control was like a physical blow to Jennifer. Thunder, much closer now, rolled and slammed against the house, a fitting accompaniment to the fury blazing in Dan's eyes. Jennifer shivered involuntarily when lightning cracked and lighted the darkness outside the floor-to-ceiling glass windows.

Unexpectedly, her thoughts rioted, and an enormous wave of guilt washed over her.

Who did she think she was, violating his privacy like this? She had come here, intent on trying to shock Dan out of his depression. But she had never intended to hurt him. He had been hurt enough. Certainly she didn't want to be the one to inflict even more.

Her eyes began to sting, and she suddenly wished she had never begun any of this. She felt as though she were losing an already tenuous grip on something very fragile, but very, very precious.

"Dan —" She heard the uncertainty in her voice. And so, apparently, had he.

"Don't stop now, Jennifer." His face could have been carved in stone.

Jennifer took a deep breath, then spilled the words out in one jumbled rush. "Everything you tried to tell me . . . it was all true."

Still he remained motionless, an impassive statue.

"You were right — about all of it."

He gave a small shake of his head and frowned. "What *are* you talking about?"

She squeezed her eyes shut for an instant, then opened them again. Through her tears, she was relieved to see that his anger appeared to be ebbing. Now he simply looked confused.

"Your journal, Dan. The things you wrote . . ."

His frown deepened. "What about it?"

"Oh, Daniel . . . it broke my heart! And that's exactly what had to happen! I had to be broken — completely broken — before God could put the pieces back together the way he wanted them. You can't mend something that isn't *broken!*"

Her words spun between them, churning into an echo that bounced across the hollow recesses of the pool house. Hesitantly, Jennifer took a step, then another, until she had closed the distance between them. Her heart was in her throat, her pulse thundering. She hadn't realized until that instant just how tightly she had been holding herself together.

Finally, when she was close enough to touch him, she stopped and stood perfectly still, raising her eyes to study with infinite caring his strong, firmly molded features. A look that was at once forlorn and hopeful now gentled his smoldering expression of moments before.

Unable to help herself, she lifted an unsteady hand and lightly touched her fingertips to his face. "Daniel . . . I understand now. What you've been trying to tell me all along. About having faith enough to trust God's love, his right to work his will in our lives . . . even when it seems that he's being unfair or that he's only doling out punishment." She paused. Perhaps it no longer made any difference, but she had to tell him everything. She had to share the life-changing explosion that had occurred in her spirit.

"In your journal," she went on, "toward the end, you wrote out Romans 8:28. 'And we know that God causes all things to work together for good to those who love God. . . .' That's the message of *Daybreak*, too, isn't it, Daniel? That God took the ugliest, most shameful symbol ever known — the cross — and turned it into glory. That what seemed to be the most awful event in history was changed into the most *important* event in history."

Even in the face of his passivity, Jennifer couldn't control her newfound joy. "Oh, Dan, don't you understand? I'm *free* now! I don't have to fight God anymore! I don't have to be angry anymore! You knew it long before I did, but I had to find it out for myself! And I did! Because of *you!* It was all there, in your journal — and in your musical, *Daybreak.*"

For a long moment, it was as though he would never move again, and Jennifer dropped her hand away from his face, letting it fall to her side in reluctant defeat.

"Maybe it doesn't matter anymore," she said in a near whisper, agony straining her voice. "But I just had to tell you." Her final words were nearly lost in the repeated blows of thunder that shook the windows of the house.

Dan's sightless eyes slowly filled with tears, and he tried to turn away from her. But Jennifer saw and grasped his shoulders with both hands, holding him. "No — don't turn away from me, Dan! Don't shut me out, please."

Had she caused the grief that washed across his face when he turned back to her? "Jennifer . . . I can't —" He swallowed with obvious difficulty. "You deserve so much more than I can give you."

"I don't *want* anything more than you can give me!" Jennifer cried. "I just want *you*." She studied him, her heart filled with love and determination. "I want to be your wife, Dan."

"Jennifer, don't you understand?" he said, misery lacing his words. "I can't look after you the way a man should." His despair was almost tangible. "I couldn't even protect an innocent little boy . . . or my own dog. That could have been *you* that day! You could have taken the bullets meant for me — and I wouldn't even have known you were in danger!"

The words exploded from him, a harsh,

agonized cry that stunned Jennifer into momentary silence.

She stared at him, understanding finally dawning. "Is *that* what's wrong?"

He didn't answer.

"It *is,* isn't it? You're punishing yourself! Because you tried to bait this lunatic to come after you in order to protect me. And then Jason and Sunny got hurt —"

He grabbed her arm in an almost painful vise. "*Yes!* And *I* caused it! It was my stupid pride, my stubbornness!" Abruptly, as though he realized he might be hurting her, he gentled his grasp on her arm.

"I thought I could manage it," he said harshly. "That's always been my way. To manage things on my own."

His jaw tensed and he shook his head at Jennifer's small cry of protest. "I thought, after the accident, that I'd finally gotten rid of that insufferable pride of mine. I even reached the point where I could actually accept help from people." He gave a nasty, short laugh. "You'd expect me to have a healthy dose of humility after I had to learn to eat and brush my teeth all over again, wouldn't you?"

Tears trickled slowly down Jennifer's cheeks as, outside, the sky finally released its pent-up deluge amid the growling thunder and flashing lightning.

"Then you came along." Dan's gentle smile of wonder — the first sign of his former tenderness Jennifer had seen in days — nearly broke her heart. "And suddenly I needed my pride back all over again." He reached out a tenuous hand to lightly graze one side of her face. "I wanted to be . . . enough for you, don't you understand? I wanted to be everything you thought I was — a giant."

Jennifer blanched. It was true. That's exactly what she had made of him in her mind. A giant of a man . . . even a spiritual giant.

His smile now turned bitter. "I may have made a halfhearted attempt to convince you I wasn't the man you thought I was. But the truth of the matter was that I enjoyed your fantasy. I wanted to be *exactly* what you thought I was. Strong. Capable. In charge. It didn't take too long for the old stubborn pride to rear its head again. I was determined to have a — *normal* relationship with you. Love. Marriage. A family. I wanted it all. I wanted to be everything you wanted me to be. And all the while, I knew I was asking for the impossible."

Jennifer closed her eyes. When she could finally bring herself to look at him again, her heart wrenched to see that tears were now falling freely down his face.

"Oh, Dan," she murmured with dismay, "you *are* everything I want, can't you understand that? *I want you* . . . exactly as you are. You say you couldn't protect a little boy or your own dog. But Dan . . . I'm *neither*. I'm a grown woman. You don't have to watch over me. I can watch over *myself*. Daniel — I don't need you to *protect* me. I need you to *love* me!"

Somehow she made her way into his arms. She felt his strong shoulders slump. He leaned against her, burying his face in her hair . . . and he wept.

Jennifer now fully understood his former pain and his near-ruin, the hopelessness that had very nearly defeated and destroyed him five years before. Her face was soaked with his tears and her own, and she was blind now, too, her vision blurred by their mingled tears. Outside, the night sky wept with them, and the mountain roared as though in its own agony. But Jennifer knew nothing except the man whose hurt she now tried to absorb into her own soul. She held him as tenderly as she would have a child, promising him silently that he would never again bear his pain alone.

And she knew then, as she could never have known before, how it must have been for him after the accident. She saw with a startling clarity how incredibly wrong she had been about the man who now wept in her arms. She saw how weak he must have been, and she realized for the first time the infinite amount of strength the Lord had given him, the awesome quality of faith God had woven from that weakness. She saw how very far her beloved had actually come . . . such a long, hard way.

"Jennifer . . . I need you. . . ."

She nodded, and murmured softly against his bearded cheek.

"You make me whole . . . you make me a man again. . . ."

"I love you, Daniel. . . ."

"You really will marry me?"

"Oh, yes, love, of course I'll marry you."

"Soon . . . ?"

"Whenever you say. . . ."

The fury outside the house muted the shrill ringing of the telephone. "Dan — the phone —"

Ever so slowly, he lifted his head and wiped the dampness from his eyes with the back of his arm. "Would you get it?"

Moving reluctantly out of his embrace, Jennifer walked to the wall phone and lifted the receiver.

It was Pauline. As soon as Jennifer answered, Dan's mother exploded with the good news. "Jennifer — Jason is conscious! He's asking for Dan! Lucas just called. Tell Dan that Jason is going to be all right!"

The excitement in her voice carried across to Dan. Jennifer saw him whisper, *"Thank you . . . thank you, Father."*

"Yes, of course, I'll drive him to the hospital," Jennifer said into the receiver as she watched Dan begin to nod. "Yes, we'll go right away!"

By the time she hung up, Dan was beside her, his arms around her. He kissed her lightly, saying, "I'll get dressed. While I change, why don't you tell Rick he can go, that we're going to leave? There's no point in his staying here without us."

Dan smiled — his old smile, the one Jennifer loved to distraction — and she knew that everything was going to be all right. It really was.

TWENTY-ONE

Jennifer leaned out the door to watch the patrol car pull out of the driveway. The wind-driven rain sprayed her face, and she was about to duck back inside when something caught her attention.

The headlights of the patrol car flashed across the east side of the house, momentarily illuminating the dense grove of pine trees only yards away. Jennifer stuck her head out even farther, ignoring the rain. She had seen something, she was sure of it, out there among the trees. Craning her neck as far as possible, she squinted into the darkness. But the lights from the patrol car were gone now, and she could see nothing but rain-swept shadows.

Still, she waited uneasily, trying for another glimpse of whatever she thought she had seen. Suddenly, an eerie blue-white glow framed the entire lot, followed by a roll of insistent thunderclaps. Jennifer winced, hunching her shoulders and squeezing her eyes shut — and missing the opportunity to get another look at the lightning-illumined field.

She shook her head in self-disgust as she jumped back inside and shut the door behind her. If she wanted to see anything, she had to keep her eyes *open*.

She stood there for a moment, her back against the door, trying to shake off her fear of the storm. Finally, she turned and started back toward the pool house.

She had just begun to breathe a little easier when a dazzling bolt of lightning nailed the ground outside the window to her right. She stopped dead, riveted by the iridescent explosion, then screamed at the boom of thunder that shook the mountain and plunged the house into total darkness.

Jennifer's blood froze. For one breathless moment, she could do nothing but stand motionless, rigid with fear.

The darkness around her was as thick as ink. She felt light-headed and hoped she wasn't going to pass out. She had to get back to Dan, to tell him about the lights going out.

But it wouldn't matter to Dan that the lights were out, she thought fleetingly. It would only matter to *her*.

She pushed a fist against her mouth, then dropped it, and clenched her hands tightly together. After a moment, she began to grope her way toward the open door of the pool house. She stumbled in the darkness, grazing her hip against the kitchen counter and kicking Sunny's food bowl across the floor.

Finally she grabbed the doorframe and stopped just inside the entrance, peering down the length of the pool.

"Dan?" She squinted into the warm dampness of the room. "Dan, the power's out. Should I call —"

The question died on her lips. She halted in midstep, her heart hammering with a vengeance. Lightning streaked, over and over again, revealing two shadows close to the door of the dressing room. On the other wall, the outside door stood open, an ominous, gaping black hole. Jennifer realized that one of the shadows — the larger one — was Dan. He appeared to be facing the wall, while the other shadow pushed against him.

Disoriented, Jennifer struggled to take in the scene in front of her. Another flash of lightning illuminated the pool house, and now she realized that Dan was pinned against the wall, with a man holding a gun at his back!

Too terrified to be cautious, she screamed. The gun-wielding man whirled toward her, his corpselike face illuminated for a dazzling instant, framed for all time in her memory. It was the same cadaverous face she had seen peering in her kitchen window!

She lunged forward, intent only on helping Dan. The man waved the gun, took a wild shot at her, and Jennifer dropped to the floor. She lay there, panicked, watching as Dan pivoted around and snaked his foot out in a low kick that knocked his assailant off-balance and sent him sprawling, arms waving, into the pool. The gun sailed out of his hand and went bouncing over the tiled floor, echoing loudly all the way down the room.

Jennifer clambered to her knees and lunged toward Dan. But she stopped dead when he shouted, *"Jennifer — get the gun!"*

Jennifer's gaze scanned the floor in search of the gun. She saw it, lying only inches from the rim of the pool. Glancing back at Dan, she saw him shrug out of his robe and slide smoothly into the water. He was going after his assailant!

Her mind felt numb. She couldn't think. A tight thread of hysteria threatened to snap somewhere inside her, and she was able to hold onto her reason only by sheer force of will — and the awareness that Daniel was alone in the pool with a madman.

"Daniel, what are you *doing?* I'm coming in, too! You can't see where he —"

"No!" he shouted over his shoulder. "I can't keep track of him *and* you! Just stay

quiet so I can hear — and *get the gun!*"

Still Jennifer hesitated. Finally, her stomach clenching with panic, she forced herself to pick up the gun. She held it extended from her body as far as possible, staring at it as though it were something alive and extremely deadly.

Dan felt the water enfold him like a warm blanket as he pushed himself away from the side of the pool and began to quietly bob up and down, listening and waiting. Within seconds he had a fix on his assailant's location, the man must have panicked. There was no time to waste; the other might regain his senses any moment.

Dan went under the water with one smooth scissor motion and began to push forward slowly but confidently. The pressure in his ears and on his lungs was nothing in comparison to the weight of desperation closing in on him.

Who *was* this lunatic, anyway? Someone he knew? What had he ever done to evoke this kind of hatred in the man?

The muffled exclamations above the surface of the water were much louder now. Dan began to feel the current lapping against his face from the other's thrashing movements. He knew he was close. Very close.

He also knew he had all the advantages for a few more seconds, at least. The sensation was rare, but exhilarating. For years he had lived with the feeling of always being at a disadvantage. He liked the idea of being in control for a change. There was also the fact that the other man was fully clothed, while he was still in his swim trunks. The weight of his assailant's soggy clothing would go against him.

Best of all, Dan thought, the power was out. His adversary would be as much in the dark as *he* was. And he had smelled alcohol on the man. If his reflexes were diminished, that would only give Dan even more of an advantage.

He swam quietly, feeling a change in the ripples as he went. Apparently, the man had begun to move away. His cries sounded farther out, and the current from the churning of the water had also begun to drift off. Dan followed the movement and the sound as closely as he dared, staying under the water and remaining totally quiet.

Until at last he knew he had him.

Dan roared up through the water in one explosive motion, grappling for his assailant. He took him from behind, raising his arms directly above the man's head and pushing him down into the water. The man tried to wave his arms. He cursed and shrieked, striking Dan in the face several times before catching him in the midriff with his elbow.

But Dan was much bigger and in far better condition. Every move the other made was in vain. Finally, with one large, powerful shove, Dan plunged him under the water and followed him down.

The man tried to fight, but was quickly pulled to the bottom by the weight of his clothes and his own panic. Dan refused to let him go. He followed him to the bottom and efficiently locked an iron forearm around his neck in a relentless hold.

As her eyes adjusted to the darkness, Jennifer stood by the side of the pool, staring with terror into the water. She could make out dark shadows of movement beneath the surface, but nothing else. Trembling, she gripped the gun, steadying it with her other hand.

They had been below for what seemed like hours. She waited, scarcely breathing. She should call the police, but she couldn't move until she knew that Dan was all right. If they didn't come up in the next few seconds, she was going in. She even kicked her tennis shoes off in preparation.

How much longer should she wait? How

long could they stay down?

She screamed and nearly dropped the gun when a wave of water sprayed her in the face as both men suddenly broke above the surface. Weak with relief, she saw Dan swim to the side of the pool, dragging the other man along with him. When he reached the pool wall, Dan hauled himself partly up out of the water, holding his assailant securely with one arm until he could pull him the rest of the way out.

"Jennifer —"

She was already beside him. "Daniel! Are you all right?"

She stopped when light flared as the electricity suddenly returned. "Dan, the lights!" she exclaimed. "The lights are back on!"

Dan was panting heavily with exertion. "Good! Take a look at this guy. Who is he anyway? Do you recognize him?"

Jennifer was still shaking. "I don't know his name, but he's the same man who was at my door the other night."

Dan nodded as if he weren't surprised. Flipping the still unconscious man over onto his back, he knelt beside him and lowered his head to listen to his chest. "He swallowed most of the pool. I'm going to have to pump him out."

He raised the man's head and checked his

airway, then flipped him — none too gently, Jennifer noticed — onto his stomach and began applying firm pressure on his back to pump the water from his lungs.

"Jennifer, you'd better call the police."

Jennifer carefully placed the gun on the table, then ran to the poolside phone to dial the police. Once she had delivered her message, practically screaming into the receiver, she hurried back to Dan, going to her knees to see if she could help. But the man was already gulping and coughing up water.

"Check his pockets, Jennifer. I want to know who he is," Dan told her as he continued to knead the man's back.

Jennifer pulled a soaked, ruined billfold out of the back pocket of the man's khaki work pants and opened it. The contents were soaked and her hands were trembling, but she finally managed to separate the driver's license from the other papers. "OK," she muttered, "here's his license. Let's see —" Jennifer stared down at the wet, laminated card and made a strangled sound of disbelief.

TWENTY-TWO

Daniel — it's *Caleb Arbegunst!* Jim's father!"

Dan froze in midmotion. Beneath his hands, the man spewed out water and coughed convulsively. *"Caleb?* Are you sure?"

"That's what it says!" Jennifer continued to stare down at the license for a moment, then scanned the other papers in his wallet. "Yes — here's a credit card. And . . . here's some kind of social services I.D. They all say the same thing. But *why,* Dan? What does Caleb Arbegunst have against *you?"*

He shook his head. "I hardly even know the man! I had only seen him once before the accident, and I haven't talked to him since."

Jennifer had nearly forgotten that Caleb Arbegunst had been with the teenage boy who hit Dan's car and caused his blindness. Still, what possible reason could he have for trying to kill Dan?

"It doesn't make any sense," Dan said, his voice puzzled as he rolled Arbegunst over onto his back. "The man is a virtual stranger to me. I —"

Suddenly he stopped, and Jennifer watched in horror as his face contorted in pain. "Dan! What is it? What's wrong?"

He seemed riveted in place, his face frozen in a look of anguish. He started to tremble, and Jennifer almost panicked, afraid he might be going into shock.

Seeing the robe he had tossed by the side of the pool, she scrambled to her feet and went after it. She returned, draping it around Dan's shoulders.

She knelt down beside him, watching him closely. Finally the tremor racking his body began to subside. He shook his head back and forth as if trying to clear his mind. "Something — about the nightmare," he said, then stopped. His shoulders slumped, and he frowned as he grazed the fingers of one hand over the scar at his eyebrow. "I can't think. . . ." His voice drifted off.

They both jumped in surprise when the man between them stirred and twisted, then began to flail his arms. His bloodshot eyes were wild and disoriented, his soaked clothing plastered to his emaciated body.

Dan quickly pinned him to the floor and held him there. Arbegunst thrashed, twisting his head from side to side as he tried to free himself from Dan's grip. He cursed and shrieked at them as he struggled to break free.

Jennifer's stomach knotted as she watched

them. When she saw Dan begin to shake again, she laid her hand on his forearm, thinking to steady him. He didn't seem to be hurt, but he was obviously in the grip of some kind of emotional storm she couldn't comprehend.

Suddenly the insane babbling from the man on the floor penetrated her consciousness.

". . . should have killed you the first time . . . knew it. Knew you'd cause trouble. . . ."

Dan choked off an exclamation and frowned, listening.

"What trouble, Caleb? What kind of trouble?" he prompted.

Arbegunst went on muttering in a crazed monotone. "Just waitin' on me, weren't you . . . just bidin' your time to ruin me, so you could take my kid . . . thought you'd drive me nuts, didn't you, then you could have my boy. . . ."

Jennifer looked at Dan and saw his jaw tighten even more as he bent low over Caleb Arbegunst.

"Daniel — what is he talking about?"

Dan waved off her words. "Waiting on *what*, Caleb?"

"All these years, you knew . . . just waitin' to tell, tryin' to make me crazy, tryin' to take my boy. Well, you ain't gonna get him. I'll shut you up for good this time, Kaine. . . ."

Dan pressed him harder to the floor. "Tell what, Caleb? What is it you think I'm going to tell?"

Jennifer framed her face with both hands in sick horror and bewilderment. She looked from Dan, whose face was a mask of self-control, down to Arbegunst, shaking and thrashing in weak futility.

"You saw me . . . you knew I was drivin' that night. They said you couldn't remember anything, but I knew better. Your memory came back a long time ago, you were just waitin' to tell. You waited so you could get my boy, didn't you? You went and gave him that job, coddled him, took him places, let him swim in your big, fancy pool. . . ."

"Driving?" Daniel echoed hoarsely. "*You* were driving . . . the night of the accident? Not the boy?"

Arbegunst uttered an ugly snort, and Jennifer felt suddenly nauseous, as much from the stench of alcohol as the emotional maelstrom.

"I wouldn't let one of those no-good punks drive my truck," Arbegunst snorted. "He wanted to . . . said I was drunk. I wasn't drunk, never been drunk on the road . . . I'd had a few beers waiting for him, that was all. Wasn't drunk. . . ."

Jennifer heard no more, the rest of his words lost to her as she reached out to grasp Dan's arm. She felt dazed and sickened by what she'd just heard. The man was admitting what he thought Dan already knew. But Jennifer took one look at Dan's face and realized that Dan *didn't* know. He had *never* known!

"Dan . . . does he mean what I think he does?"

Her question fell between them, dying quickly in the silence. Even the storm outside was subsiding, nothing left of it except a few weak spurts of lightning and the sound of muffled thunder moving off into the distance. The earlier torrential rain had turned to a gentle, rhythmic patter, almost hypnotic in its steady thrum against the metal roof.

Jennifer continued to watch Dan, fearful of what he might do. His grasp on Arbegunst never faltered. He was like a kneeling statue, frozen in place. The erratic rhythm of his breathing, the thin line of perspiration that had begun to drape itself along the ridge above his dark brows, the sudden, uncharacteristic paleness that settled over his face were the only hints of the storm that might be gathering in his soul.

"You were driving the truck, Caleb?" His voice was ominously quiet. "Not the boy?"

Jennifer had never had such an urge to lash out and strike a man as she did when she heard the high-pitched explosion of laughter that ripped from Caleb Arbegunst's mouth.

"Dumb kid, tried to grab the wheel from me . . . coulda got us both killed. . . ."

Dan's face contorted into a thunderous mask of rage. He moved his hands from Arbegunst's shoulders to his neck, and Jennifer gasped when she saw his fingers clench and unclench. "Dan —"

"The boy *was* killed, you drunken —" Suddenly Dan stopped, shook himself almost violently, and Jennifer saw his hands tighten once, then again, before dropping back to Caleb Arbegunst's shoulders.

"You put the boy under the wheel — after the crash." He made it a statement, not a question.

"Yeah . . . you were out cold . . . you didn't see me, nobody saw me. He was just a scrawny kid; I pushed him right under the wheel. Nobody ever knew. Even poured whiskey on him so they'd think he was drunk. They didn't even check me out. Nobody saw. Nobody knew . . ." His red-rimmed, watery eyes cleared and focused on Dan. "Except you."

Jennifer watched Dan, afraid of what he

272

might do. His features were unreadable. "No, Caleb," he said, his voice chillingly quiet. "I never knew. No one knew but you. Until now."

Slowly, little by little, the man on the floor quieted, the insanity temporarily stilled. He stared up at Dan, as if unable to grasp or accept the truth of what he had heard.

"You're lyin'! You knew — you always knew! You wanted to make me crazy . . . you wanted my boy. . . ."

Dan shook his head in a sad, hopeless gesture. "You poor fool," he murmured softly. "You sold out your whole life — even your own son — for a bottle of temporary escape and a soul full of guilt."

Still holding Arbegunst to the floor, Dan looked like a man coming out from under a long sleep.

"I never knew," he said again. "I had nothing to go on except a nightmare. A bad dream that never seemed to end. Your secret would probably have been safe for a lifetime."

Arbegunst twisted his head back and forth in violent denial. "No, you knew . . . you always knew. You even said on the radio you knew who I was. . . ."

Dan didn't answer right away. When he did, his tone held a note of surprise. "I wasn't talking about the accident. I was just trying to bait you, draw you out into the open so you'd make a move. And then I nearly caused Jason and Sunny to get killed. No," he said once more, very softly. "You were the only one who knew the truth, Caleb."

They heard the sirens then, wailing up the mountain. Jennifer drew her first long breath in what seemed like hours and rose trembling to her feet to open the front door for the police.

But Gabe was already through the door, using the key he always carried. He blasted through the entrance to the pool house, nearly knocking Jennifer to the floor in his effort to reach Dan. "What happened — what's going on? The police chased me all the way up here!"

Jennifer saw with relief that there was a ghost of a smile on Dan's face when he answered. "Relax, buddy — everything's under control."

At that moment, two police officers brandishing revolvers charged in behind Gabe. Dan hauled himself to his feet and, after turning Caleb Arbegunst over to the police, slipped into his robe.

Almost at once, Gabe began shooting questions at Dan, who gave him a few brief but concise answers, then held up a restraining hand. "I need a minute. Take everyone into the house and leave me alone, would you?"

Jennifer thought he sounded — and looked — extremely weary. Gabe darted a questioning look at her, and she managed a weak but reassuring smile.

Dan pulled in a long breath, then said again, "I need to be alone . . . just for a few minutes. Please?" He paused, then added, "Then if someone will take me, I want to go to Jason."

"Isn't anyone going to tell me what's happened?" Gabe's voice was decidedly testy.

"Jennifer," said Dan, "talk to the man, would you? I'm going to change into some dry clothes."

Jennifer stood with Gabe and watched Dan as he turned and began walking slowly toward the dressing room. She thought with admiration that Daniel Kaine was the only man she had ever known who could wear a terry cloth beach wrap with as much style as a royal robe.

He went on walking, her stricken prince, and she saw his slumped shoulders gradually lift and finally straighten in the familiar mantle of determined strength he wore so easily and so well.

Abruptly, he stopped beside the aluminum table near the pool and after a slight hesitation picked up the cane he had left there. For a moment he stood unmoving, as if he were making a decision. Then, with a jaunty flick of his wrist, he tossed the cane lightly into the air, caught it easily on its descent, and sent it sailing smoothly into the deepest part of the pool.

Jennifer couldn't see his face, only his back. But she knew beyond a doubt he was wearing the vagabond grin she had grown to love so well.

EPILOGUE

Daniel felt the warmth, the excitement, and the special hush of hope in the sanctuary unique to Easter Sunday. He heard the choir stir slightly, readying themselves for the finale of *Daybreak*.

As Jennifer began the solo, he wondered if he would ever find it possible to separate that rich and glorious singing voice of hers from the low, endearing speaking voice of the woman he loved.

Just as it had during rehearsals, her voice once again moved him to worship. He realized anew that one of the miracles of her gift, one of the wonders of her voice, was the way the Lord seemed to lift it, temporarily, above human things, using it to bring people to their knees in simple worship. For the next few moments, she would no longer be his Jennifer, his beloved, but instead, an instrument of praise.

With that thought, he straightened his shoulders and readied himself for what he knew he and the entire congregation were about to experience. He smiled to himself in anticipation and silently thanked his Lord for all the doors that had been closed . . . and all the new doors that had been opened

. . . to lead Jennifer to this place — to *him,* to the music, and to her new peace of spirit.

Dan gave thanks, as he so often had, that her voice, deemed less than enough for operatic stage, was so wonderfully perfect for the Lord's purposes. And then he simply listened and let his own spirit soar along with the voice and the music. . . .

Slowly, Jennifer returned from the place the music had taken her. She opened her eyes and saw Dan standing there, smiling to himself, yet smiling at her, too, and she knew once more that, even though he couldn't see her face, he was seeing her heart. He was looking deep inside her, seeing what was there and loving what he saw.

As she held the last note and heard it echo and fade into the hushed sanctuary, she thanked her God for the light he had poured into her heart, into her spirit . . . and into their love, hers and Daniel's.

She smiled a little when the choir breathed a collective sigh with the congregation, and Lyss, standing next to her, squeezed her hand. At the end of the row, Gabe gave her an uncommonly serious nod of affirmation.

She watched the effect of the music gradually lift away from the congregation, seeing many of them dry their eyes before flinging themselves to their feet in a combined accolade to their God, to the choir — and to Daniel.

She saw the proud, happy faces of her dad and Loren smiling up at her. And she watched little Jason — her future son — grin from ear to ear as he waved eagerly to her. She smiled at Jim Arbegunst, seated between Dan's parents, who now had temporary custody of the boy. She thought it was the first time she had ever seen Jim looking happy and healthy and unafraid.

Her eyes filled when she saw Dan finally relax his shoulders from the monumental effort into which he had poured so much of his heart and soul. He wiped a handkerchief across his forehead and dabbed at his cheeks. Then he turned around to the congregation and raised one hand in a sweeping motion of tribute to the choir and the large wooden cross that stood behind them. Finally, he turned back to the choir, gently smiling in Jennifer's direction . . . and her spirit started to sing all over again.

As the choir began to leave the platform, she waited for Dan. Together the two of them, along with Sunny, walked down the aisle, following the choir out while the congregation waited. When they were almost to the door, Dan took her hand and placed it snugly on his forearm, covering it with his own.

"Is the sun shining this morning, love?"

Jennifer glanced up at his smiling face, then down at her hand and the diamond solitaire gleaming there. The ring captured a sunbeam, a rainbow of light streaking in through the stained-glass window nearby.

"Oh, yes, Daniel," she replied, glancing from her ring up to him. "The sun is definitely shining this morning."